Spotli

Sammy Boswell

Spotlight

1st Edition (March 28 2023)

ISBN: [9798379095086]

Makes me that much stronger

Makes me work a little bit harder

Makes me that much wiser

So thanks for making me a fighter

Christina Aguilera

1

A cold and windy winter morning in February.
A wall of clouds fills the sky, reflecting onto the stone
beach. It was usual scenery for Brighton at this time of
year: a deserted fairground, abandoned beach huts, litter
everywhere. This was the life I had known all my life - I
had barely left Brighton before. To clarify, I am eighteen
years old and left school at the end of last year. I guess I
lack a lot of life experience, but as a family we never had
any money to spend on lavish trips abroad.

It was a Tuesday afternoon, and usually I'd be working
down at the leisure centre, but I had quit my job just two
weeks prior. The fact they were only paying me five
pounds an hour was one reason, but also, I was moving
into my cousin's flat up in London! A daunting move for
someone who hadn't left Brighton for her whole life - you
could call me a small-town girl but Brighton is quite a big
place! I'm not sure what London will be like - I don't
know what to expect. I see it all the time on the TV - the
most memorable for me is seeing the fireworks on New
year's, especially as we have just seen in the new
millennium.

I walk up to the desolate pier, a stark contrast to what it is
normally like in the summer. I have so many memories
from this pier - getting ice cream when I was a child from
the van down the end, to having my first kiss with a boy

named George when I was thirteen. All these memories washed over me in a split-second as out of the corner of my eye, I clocked my best friend Alexandra walking along - she was wearing a grey hoodie and matching joggers and held a can of diet coke in one hand and her silver Motorola in the other. I could see her chewing what I can only presume is gum (not sure how she is drinking diet coke and chewing gum- but that's Alexandra for you!)

"Alexandra! Alexandra!" I shouted.

"Oh my god, Nicola! How are you? I feel like I haven't seen you in ages." She replied quickly. "I'm doing really well at the moment - I'm just getting everything ready for the big move this Friday."

"Oh babe, I'm really going to miss you. It's not going to be the same without you."

"I'll be back most weekends, I promise. I'm really nervous, but I can't just remain in Brighton forever, can I?"

"I guess you're right Nicola - gosh you were always the smart one out of all of us weren't you!"

We both start giggling hysterically - I'll miss this when I'm gone. I don't think a week has gone by where I haven't spent time with her or spoken to her.

"It's just going to be so different isn't it!" I exclaimed. "I genuinely don't know if it's the best idea for me to actually go through with this - or if I'm crazy."

"Well, we'll all still be here when you come back." She reassured me.

"I appreciate it, love you."

We proceeded to walk up the promenade - I was walking a step behind Alexandra, because she was five foot eight, but I was only five foot three, so I struggled to keep up with her. She pointed to turn right so we did and walked up towards the shopping centre.

"Why do you want to go to the shopping centre so bad?" I asked directly.

"I need to get some concealer, it's urgent. I ran out last week and I've had to borrow my sisters ever since. It's embarrassing to be honest, Nic!"

"Ok let's go find some then, but I need to go in a bit. I've got to get home to sort some stuff out before I leave for London."

Alexandra then ran into the first shop she saw (even though it was a clothes shop with no make-up in site). She started picking up different items.

"Do you like this?" She picked up a red low-cut dress from the rack.

"Yeah, it's nice, are you going to get it?" I replied quickly.

"Hm, no. Maybe not."

Oh god, I thought.

We're going to be here forever.

Alexandra swiftly moves onto the next rack of clothes - this time it's the jeans section. She starts picking up the jeans and resting them on the lower part of her arm. I thought to myself please don't be going to the changing rooms-

"I'm going to try these on if that's alright Nic!"
"Yes of course Alex." Secretly, I was annoyed - but I did my best to hide it, only rolling my eyes slightly when she was turned away. She strutted across the store towards the changing rooms. It was just one singular changing room with a one singular wooden bench outside it. I perched on the bench as Alexandra walked straight into the changing room locking it behind her. The door was painted an ocean blue - albeit it was painted badly because you could see the wooden undertones beneath the peeling paint.

I must have sat there for about 15 minutes before Alexandra actually came out to show me what she had been trying on. The first was a pair of black jeans matched with a black hoodie. I thought it did make her look a bit like a goth to be honest, and it didn't really suit her at all. I was torn between being honest and just being nice, but Alex would have been honest with me - so I said it how it was.
"You look a bit gothic, maybe add some colour." There was a pause, and I got a pang of worry in my stomach.
"Yeah, I thought so, I think lighter colours suit me better, don't you?"
I nodded and smiled in response. She went back into the changing rooms, and I went and fished out my phone from under the hundreds of bits of rubbish that filled my black River Island bag. My phone was quite old but it worked fine, it was a Nokia 5110 from around 1997 or 1998 - I got

it with one of my pay cheques recently. I opened it to find a text from my cousin Rochelle:

Rochelle: Hiya hun, how are you? So excited for you to come live with me! Me and Andre are so happy you're coming! Just letting you know we've got Andre's brother living with us called Romeo - he'll be sleeping in the room on the top floor, and you'll have the one on the middle floor. R xx
I quickly scanned through it and replied:
All good! Can't wait xx Nicola.

Alexandra came out of the changing room a second time - this time she looked much better. She was wearing a navy blue cut dress and it looked stunning on her.
"Wow, you look like a model Alex!"
"Really? I don't like it that much…"
"I do! It suits you a lot."
Part of me was hoping she would put all the clothes back and we would finally leave the shop. This might make me seem like a really bad friend- but don't get me wrong I love Alexandra- she just takes forever shopping!

She proceeded to go back into the changing room, this time returning with her outfit from before on.
"Where should we go next?" she asked.
"Let's get the concealer you need to get and head back home." I replied.
"That sounds good to me!"

We walked towards the beauty store and Alexandra quickly picked up a concealer and went to pay for it. Thankfully it was over quite quickly!

We walked out of the store, through the big white double doors of the shopping centre, and down the steps.
"Shall we get the bus or the train?" Alexandra turned to me.
"I'm not sure, I'm happy with either." I replied.
"Let's get the train, shall we? I'm too tired to wait for a bus."
"Same!" We both giggled at the same time.

We strolled towards the train station (which was quite a long way from the train). I looked at my watch and it read 15:24 - the train would be leaving in about eight minutes. I tried to speed up the pace, but Alexandra was too busy distracted by all the nature around the St Nicholas Park. We then rejoined Queen's Road right up to the train station.
"I am glad I bumped into you today!" I said to Alexandra.
"So am I, it was good to see you before you leave for London. How are you feeling about it?"
"I am a bit nervous; I'm not going to lie - it's completely new territory and I don't really know what to expect. I'm also really worried about how dad will cope."
My dad was a single parent of four children - I was the eldest at eighteen years old, then Kieran was fourteen, Ashleigh was eight and Carter was four. Kieran and I had

the same mum, but Ashleigh and Carter had different mums. My mum left my dad when Kieran was three and I was seven, saying she couldn't handle the pressure of looking after children anymore. She ran off with an American - I've not seen her since. It's left me with a lot of abandonment issues, and I worry constantly that the people who I trust will leave me just like she did.

"I'm sure they'll be fine, your dad is really strong. He's been a single parent for over ten years now." Alexandra tried to reassure me. "I know you don't want to leave him, but you are doing this for you. He wouldn't want to hold you back."
"I guess you're right…" I felt a wash of guilt come over me, but then thought to myself: I've done everything for my younger siblings for years - for once it's my time to put me first.

2

Back at home, I lay on my bed in the room I had lived in for the past eighteen years. My room was painted a lilac colour, with a small wooden table and a plain white chair. It was quite compact, but the highlight was a big poster of Sporty spice with her signature plastered on the bottom right side of it. I think it was from the early eras, but I can't really remember how I got it - I just knew it looked sick on the left wall! I had a small attic window that looked onto the dirty garden that hadn't been touched in months (mainly because it was February).

My bedroom was on the top floor of the house and is the only room on the top floor - it was originally an attic, but my dad managed to convert it into a bedroom when Kieran and I were really young. My dad was a talented man; he could do anything he put his mind to, but he had to stop working full time to look after the younger ones, and now he works from home as an admin assistant.

I left my room and carefully walked down the (very) steep stairs towards the ground floor. On the middle floor, Kieran had a bedroom on the left and then dad had converted a former wardrobe space into his own bedroom (which was pretty small), while the youngest two shared the original master bedroom. Now I'm thinking about it, my dad made so many sacrifices for us when we were younger. He's my rock.

I'm going to miss him so much.

I walked into the empty kitchen- it's a cream colour with a large fridge. There's a large picture of us as a family at the beach from back in 1995, and a calendar for the year 2000, decorated with different holiday destinations from across the world. My dad was in the other room, and I could hear him muttering. I tried to make out what he was saying.

"Whilst you're in there Nic, can you get me the custard creams?"

"Yeah of course dad, I'll bring them in for you."

I reached for the cupboard above my head and picked up a yellow tub sitting on the bottom shelf. Opening the lid, I pushed open the door and placed them on the coffee table.

"Thanks mate, you alright?" Dad asked.

"Yeah dad, just nervous about moving." I replied - he didn't move his eyes off the TV screen. "I don't want to go if you don't want me too."

"Don't say that Nicola. You need to live your life - the times I lived in London were the best of mine!"

"Wait… Dad, you lived in London?"

"Yeah, a long time ago. I was about your age, and I used to live in a flat up in Barnet, which I guess is quite far out of central London, but not too long on the tube. It was a great time. I used to go out every Friday and every Saturday, but this was 1980 so it's a long time ago now!"

"Oh wow! I never knew that. That's crazy."

"You will love it there, Nic - I promise. Now give me a hug!"

He leans in for a hug, and I put my arms around him while wiping the tears that are streaming down my cheeks. I squeeze him tightly before finally letting go.

Then I wipe my eyes and walk back towards the door.

"See you later, dad."

"Bye Nic, love ya."

*

I walked back up the long flight of stairs back to my bedroom and lay on my bed. I got my phone out from my bag that I'd left on the floor.

I picked it up and flipped up the front bit to fold it out. The phone flashed up a green notification which read 'three new messages'. I clicked on it:

Alexandra: Hey Nic, just wanted to say how much I loved seeing you today! You are going to smash London - always come visit us! We will have to plan your 19th birthday. A xx

I replied with: *Alexandra, I'll miss you so much. We'll have to meet up and you have to come up to London to see me! I'll be back for my birthday at the end of March xx*

I then read the other message; it was from my other friend Bonnie who I have known literally since birth. Bonnie was there through all the traumatic teenage years, and I was there for her.

Bonnie: Heyyy, do you wanna go for drinks later, i'm around! I just want to see you before you move away.

Yeh I don't see why not? Do you want to meet at the pub down my road?

I got a reply almost instantly - *Yeh that sounds cool to me! See ya at 7.*
I replied with - *Ok hun can't wait!*

I was happy to be going to see Bonnie, as I was worried I wouldn't get to see her before I left, and as she was my best friend. I went to look in my wardrobe to see if there was anything I could wear: I picked out a bright blue denim jacket - very 2000! 'Good Vibes' was spray painted on the back in green and purple. I liked it and I remember it being quite expensive, but a bit too out there just for a drink in the pub. I picked out a green jumper and paired it with a set of dark blue jeans, and decided to go with that. Casual but comfy.

The clock hit 6:45, and I walked down the stairs, got my key out of my jeans pocket and unlocked the front door to exit the house. I walked down the street towards the pub -

the street was quite steep, and you could see the beach and Hove town from the top, it was that high. Down the street, I could see Bonnie turning the corner; I locked eyes with her and shouted:

"Bonnie… Bonnie… Hii." She ran over towards me (almost being knocked down by a blue Vauxhall Corsa on the way across the road). That's why I love her though - she's so clueless sometimes! "How are you Bonnie?" She runs over and hugs me, quite tightly actually.

"I'm good, just so happy to see you. You're glowing in that outfit!"

"Aw thanks Bonnie, you look stunning as well. How is your relationship with Harry going?"

"Oh wow we definitely haven't seen each other for a long time! Well, the relationship with Harry ended a couple of weeks ago."

"Oh…How? Are you ok?"

"I ended it. His feelings definitely weren't real, I was quite sad about it, but I think I've found a new man at the garden centre I work at."

"Really? What's his name and how old is he?"

"He's called Liam and, well, he's a bit older than me. He just had his twenty-third birthday this past Friday."

"That's cool! I hope it all goes well. Have you got anything planned with him?"

"Hopefully he decides to ring me ASAP!"

Whilst we were gossiping, we walked through the big red door of the pub. The pub was called The Dolphin and had been a hangout spot for our parents- when we were young children, we used to play in the garden behind it. It was a relatively small place - basically just a bar and a couple of tables- but it was a great place to go for a drink. If I remember rightly, it definitely has become much classier than it was when I was younger - they went through a huge renovation about five years ago. They were shut for a whole year for it (which my dad was not very happy about!) but it changed completely.

"Wow, I forget how different it looks every time I walk into here." Bonnie turned to me. Her eyes then darted around the room picking out all the different features of the place. She had the fiercest orange/hazel eyes I'd ever seen; they sometimes scare me.
"Yeah same, I always remember the drab red wallpaper that looked like it was falling apart, it reminded me of a Wetherspoons!"
"Nicola! You need to be careful saying that. You never know who's listening." She laughed to herself. That did make me laugh to be fair, but I don't like being told off. I see myself as an open book and that's how I was raised. Although, it did get me in trouble sometimes.
"You're right." I rolled my eyes, but smiled at the same time.

Bonnie walked up to the bar and ordered us a cider each. I quite liked cider; it actually might be the only alcoholic drink I like. She walked back to the table and handed me one.

"Cheers!" We said in unison.

"So tell me: what's the plan for when you move to London? What are you going to do there?" Bonnie asked.

"Well, my cousin Rochelle - she's twenty-three-"

"A bit like Liam!"

"Yes! Well, she owns two hairdressers in Crystal Palace and near Beckenham Junction. She co-owns them with her husband Andre who I think is twenty-one and they've both done really well for themselves. Originally the one in Beckenham was owned by Andre's parents, but they managed to open another one when they took it on. They're loaded - they went to Thailand for their honeymoon."

"Jealous! I'd be lucky if I had a holiday in Worthing!"

"Same here. Well, Rochelle mentioned to me the last time she came down that I should come up and work as a receptionist at the salon, as they're trying to create a spa treatment centre on the upper floor. She said with my receptionist experience at the Leisure Centre, I could transfer the skills over."

"That sounds amazing Nic, I'm hoping it all goes well there. I'm so happy for you though, even though I'll miss you a lot."

We continued talking for hours, it got to about 23:30 and it was definitely time to go. Bonnie was stumbling and slightly slurring her words, so I knew it was time to drag her home. I would have called her a taxi, but I didn't have the kind of money for that, so it would be a twelve-minute walk to Bonnie's flat. I basically carried her down the hill to Kingsway, which was on the beach front. I envied Bonnie for the view her flat had, but at this moment in time, I was not happy about her flat being on the sixth floor. The sixth floor! I had to essentially drag her up the six flights of stairs to her flat. I was exhausted.

"Um, where are we?"

"We're at your flat, I need your house key if I'm going to be able to get in."

If I'm being honest, I wasn't surprised the night ended in the way it always did- but I was just happy I spent one more night with my best friend before I left.

She handed me the key - although she dropped it about five times before it ended up in my hand. It was quite a frustrating process.

"Are we in the house yet?" She slurred.

"I'm just opening the door. Be patient!"

"Ok, ok, ok, ok, ok."

I turned the key and shoved the door open. The flat was a mess, but it was actually quite big - I'm not even sure how Bonnie managed to get it for such a cheap price.

The flat had a small white kitchen on the left side, and then a sofa bed with a door to the main bedroom next to it. I dragged Bonnie into the bedroom and pulled the duvet cover up, and she basically collapsed onto it. I tucked her in and then left the room. Before I could leave, Bonnie started speaking.

"Please stay, please!"

"I've got to go Bonnie-"

"No, you're going to stay here, you can sleep on the sofa bed."

"Ok fine, I will then."

"Night Bonnie."

I got no response; she must have nodded off.

I decided to spend the next hour or so cleaning up the flat -I had an intense fear of mess. Everything I was around needed to be clean. I'm pretty sure I read something about it online about it being a disorder, but it's not very well known at the moment.

I then crashed onto the sofa bed at what must have been 1:30 in the morning. I was knackered, but I still couldn't sleep. Tomorrow was the day my life would change; I was moving to London
A new life, A new me.

3

My eyes opened; they took a second to adjust. The first
thought I had was oh god, Bonnie has managed to make
me stay at her place - right before I have to move. My
eyes flashed to the red oven timer - it was 7:30. My first
thought was to go back to sleep, but I was supposed to be
leaving for London at eleven. I was tempted to make a
quick escape for it, but I didn't want to not say bye to
Bonnie. I walked into her room quietly to see if she was
awake.

"Ouch, I have such a bad headache."

"I must have told you to lay off the booze last night, did I
not? This happens every time Bonnie!" I laughed. "Do
you want me to get you some water?"

"Yes please. That would be amazing."

I walked through to her kitchen - it may have been plain
white, but she had stuck a cute bowl of green flowers by
the window. From the window you could see Hove beach
and the glistening light blue water, although there was a
tint of green in it today (probably from all the rubbish and
algae in there).

I turned the tap on and picked up a glass from the
cupboard above my head. I filled the glass and walked

back into Bonnie's room, where I put it on her bedside table.

"I'm moving today. I'm so nervous- I don't know what to expect." I sat on the end of her bed.

"You will love it I promise, and if you hate it, you can always come home and stay at my place!"

"I might take you up on that offer if I do come back- I don't think I could go back and live with my family again."

"Sounds like a great plan B!" Bonnie reached up to grab the glass of water from her bedside table, shoved the pills at the back of her throat and took a sip. "Gross, I hate taking pills."

"Same, they always taste so horrible." I replied. Bonnie had a small green alarm clock on the other bedside table, and it read 8:00.

"Bonnie, I've got to go. I'm sorry, but I've got to make sure everything's sorted before I leave."

"Ok, bye Nikki. Thank you so much for spending the night with me. Love you."

"Love you too."

I dashed out of the apartment and ran back up the hill towards my house. I knocked on the front door twice and was greeted by dad.

"Where have you been? A message to say you weren't coming home would have been nice."

"Sorry dad, it was late, and Bonnie wanted me to stay over, so I did." He gestured for me to come in, and I

23

walked past him and went straight for the stairs. I was in desperate need of a shower. I went straight into my room and started throwing out clothes to find something to wear. After a few frustrating minutes, I picked out the usual clothes I wore and to be honest, I was fine with it - it worked.

I ran downstairs to the shower and rushed in and out within twenty minutes.

I went back upstairs and got out my suitcase that I had kept under my bed. The suitcase was quite small, so I had struggled to fit all the items I needed to take with me in it. All I really needed to do was some smart packing and just pack my essentials - Clothes, make-up, toothbrush, towels, sunglasses and a secret emergency money stash that I needed just in case I got stuck. I obviously had a smaller bag - my black River Island handbag which had my phone and my wallet and some other random stuff, that I had basically just thrown in there. I pulled the suitcase out from under my bed, picked it up, took it downstairs and left it by the door.

I walked into the kitchen, and my whole family was sitting around the table.

"We're really going to miss you, Nic." My brother Kieran said. He ran up and hugged me. I was a bit stunned - he had never ever hugged me in my life.

"Nicola, I love you, please come back and see us all the time." Ashleigh ran up to me, she looked like she was about to cry. She handed me a card she had drawn.

"Aw, Ashleigh, I love it so much. Thank you!" I could feel myself welling up.

And then finally, my dad came up to me.

"Smash it, I know you will. Love you always."

"Thanks, I love you all so, so much - I'm going to miss you all." I turned away towards the door. "I'll see you all later, I'll keep you in the loop with everything that's going on, I promise."

I walked towards the door, my eyes filling with tears. I needed to cry, but I just wasn't ready to. I opened the door and shouted "Bye, I'll see you all soon!" and then the door shut behind me.

I walked out of the house and turned back once to stare back at it.

That's when it hit me - this was the start of my adult life.

4

I walked towards the train station - Hove station was quite
a big station for quite a small place. I went up to the ticket
machine outside of the building, and ordered a ticket to
London Victoria. £13? What a rip off! That would have
been over two and a half hours at my Leisure centre job! I
got on the train at 11:20 and it was almost packed. I had to
stand, which was annoying, but I put up with it. The
carriage was bleak and green. On a few of the seats you
could see dried gum and food stains - it looked like it
hadn't been cleaned in forever.

Once the train had stopped in Brighton, most of the
carriage had emptied out, so I sat on a four-seater section
so I could fit all my bags in. We passed through Brighton,
up towards Preston Park and then into the South Downs.
This had to have been the furthest I had ever been out of
Brighton already, and we had only just got into Redhill.

I looked out of the window to see a massive motorway
and a road sign saying "M25". I knew this was the road
distinguishing London and the rest of the UK - it dawned
on me that there was no turning back, this was my new
life. After we passed the M25, we basically zoomed into
London passing through Croydon, Clapham Junction and
then into London Victoria. I stepped off the train, almost

falling through the gap in the process (kind of traumatic), but I tried to play it off like it didn't happen. I walked towards the barriers and put my ticket through so that I could check the departure board to see when the next train heading towards Beckenham Junction was: it was at 13:04, so in about twenty-five minutes.

By this point, I hadn't eaten anything all day, so I was really hungry. I went into the Boots that was across from the barriers and picked up a Chicken Caesar Salad. This was definitely one of my most healthy choices, but I knew that I was in London now and everyone was healthy in London- I wanted to follow the trend. Then I realised the difference in price when I scanned through the salad on the self-checkout - £3.50? Rip off.

I walked over to the platform my train was on and crossed over to the ticket machine to get my second ticket (I didn't realise you could just buy one combined ticket for both journeys). The train was just pulling into Victoria as I walked towards it. I boarded the train - it was relatively similar to the first train I had got on, but this one felt a lot cleaner than the first one. I lugged my suitcase along the aisle of the train towards a seat with more space. I managed to find one near the back end of the train and sat down.

The train departed Victoria just on time and was pretty much non-stop to Beckenham Junction. From the window, I could see all the different scenes of London. There were built up areas, but also there were a lot of green areas and parks. We must have pulled into Beckenham at around 13:45, and I messaged Rochelle to say I had arrived:

Hey Rochelle, my train has just pulled into Beckenham Junction, where do I go from here?

I got a response within a minute of sending the message.

Nic! So glad you've made it. We've sent Romeo out to get you because Andre and I are at the salon in CP today but we'll be home before 6 and we'll order a takeaway when we get home! Can't wait to see you. R xx

I was confused, because I didn't know what Romeo looked like at all. I was quite scared, but I thought he might be good-looking, and that kept me going. I walked out of the station doors and could see a man - probably in his mid-20s- dressed in a black tracksuit with his arm in a cast. He had dirty blonde hair and was about 6ft 2. He had really nice cheekbones and electric green eyes. He was gorgeous. I was praying this was going to be Romeo.

"You must be Nicola- Hi, I'm Romeo."
He walked up to me. It was a bit awkward for a moment.
"Yes, hey Romeo. H-how are you doing?"
"I'm good, do you want to follow me? I'll show you where Rochelle and Andre's house is. It's really nice."

"That would be great thankyou- I've never been to London!" I was hoping that he couldn't hear the nervousness in my voice.

"Really? That's crazy! You're going to love it; I promise you. I miss London every time I go back home."

"Where do you usually live?"

"Newcastle." He turned to me and smiled.

"Wow, what do you do in Newcastle?"

"I am a footballer - although not a very good one apparently, as you might be able to tell from the wrist."

"What happened to it, is it broken?"

"Yeah- I'm out for six weeks, maybe more, so I had to escape the media storm at home and come down here, so Andre decided to invite me to stay with him for a bit. I enjoy living with them, it's much more chilled out."

"In the media? Are you famous?"

"Not really famous, the papers just like to harass me on a daily basis- it's a bit different up there. If you play badly, they hound you. If you're spotted with a girl, they will hound you and the girl. If you go out partying, the pictures will be in the papers the next day."

"Wow, I've never met anyone who's famous before - this is quite crazy!" We continued to walk along the Beckenham high street passing all the chain shops. It kind of reminded me of being back in Brighton, as all the shops were the same. It gave me a sense of warmth seeing River Island and New Look on the high street.

"So, Nicola… What's your story?" Romeo turned to me.

"Well, I live quite a boring life compared to you, I guess. I live in Brighton with my family, I worked as a receptionist for a couple of years after I left school, and to be honest I've never been outside of my hometown before." I replied anxiously.

"That's cool, do you have any siblings?"

"Yeah, I have three siblings - two brothers and a sister. What about you?"

"Well obviously I have Andre, he's my little brother, but I have another sister who is similar to your age. Her name is Nadine."

"Are you close with her?"

"Yeah, I love her. I'll protect her against anything. Oh look - this is their house."

The house was so pretty, it was a Victorian townhouse and had ivy wrapped around its purple door. I followed Romeo through the front door, and it was like stepping into a show home. Not a speck of dust or dirt in sight. The kitchen was completely white- there was not a different shade of colour in the whole room. They had bifold doors looking onto a pristinely kept garden, with a small patio and astroturf stretching out to the fence.

"It's so clean in here- I've never seen anything like it!"

"I'm going to be honest, Nicola? Nikki?"

"I don't mind, Nikki is good." I laughed awkwardly. I really hoped he couldn't tell how nervous and awkward I was, I just hoped he liked me.

"Well, Nikki. The only reason it's really clean is because of Rochelle. I know for a fact my brother does not take part in any of the cleaning!"

He laughed, and I think he waited for me to laugh too, but I just couldn't force it out of me. I was too awkward, so I cracked up an attempt at a smile (I can't imagine it looked genuine).

"Come on, I'll show you to your room- you'll love it!" He gestured towards the stairs, and I followed him up. The number of stairs reminded me of home, especially as he was leading me up to the top floor. Once we got there, there were three rooms - one was a bathroom and then two bedrooms. Romeo gestured to the left and said, "That's my room over there" and then pointed to the right and said, "That one is yours." We both walked into the room, and I put my suitcase down beside my bed. The bed was a broad double bed - the biggest bed I think I've ever seen! The walls were white, like much of the house was. Opposite the bed was a big window looking out onto the Beckenham 'skyline', with bright blue curtains either side.

"Right, I'll leave you to it- if you have any issues, I'll be downstairs in the living room watching the football."
"Thank you."
"My pleasure- I think we're going to have quite a lot of fun being neighbours for a few weeks."
As soon as he shut the door, I collapsed onto my bed. All I could think about was Rome: Romeo was gorgeous, he

was a footballer, he was everything I had ever wanted in a man and to top it all off- I knew he was probably not attracted to me. A seven-year age gap - but when has that stopped anyone?

I gazed out of the window, and realised how much my life has changed in a day. I was in London- It felt like I had become an adult overnight. As I started to unpack my clothes, I realised I was on my own - dad wasn't there to help me with anything.

I could hear a key through the door, and Romeo shouted up to me "Nicola...Nicola! Come downstairs. Andre and Rochelle are home!"
I rushed down the stairs to see the two of them at the door. Andre looked just like his brother- just an inch or two shorter. Rochelle had long curly brown hair and must have been about five foot six. She ran straight up to me and hugged me.
"I am so glad you're staying with us, finally another girl in the house!"
"Thanks so much for having me Roch -I can't wait to start working at the salon!"
"We can't wait to have you working there- you're going to love it!" Andre then came up to me and gave me a hug.
"I'm Andre- I'm so glad you've come to stay with us." He then walked towards the kitchen, where Rochelle ushered Romeo and I to follow.

We all sat down at the kitchen table, Andre next to Rochelle and Romeo next to me. I was happy to be sitting next to Romeo, but I didn't want to look like I was too excited.

"What takeaway do you all want?" Andre asked.

I piped up first, "I don't mind- I'm happy with anything." I smiled, and Andre smiled back at me.

"I vote pizza!" Andre shouted.

"Same!" Rochelle added.

"Ok, let's get pizza then- what do you all want?"

"I want a margarita; I know it's plain but it's my favourite." Rochelle proclaimed.

"I'll get a tuna one please." Andre requested.

"Hm… I'll have a margarita as well, thank you so much!"

"I'll just go ring the pizza place up now, you guys make yourselves comfortable."

This was the first time I was sitting having dinner with people who weren't my friends or my family. Rochelle might have been my cousin, but I barely knew her. When she lived down in Worthing, I used to see her maybe three to four times a year. Don't get me wrong, I was so grateful and happy to be living with her, but it all felt a bit daunting and like a different world. Then I had this god of a man next to me - secretly, I hoped he fancied me back, but I can't imagine he did - I was only eighteen after all.

Andre walked back into the room. "They'll be thirty minutes max." He smiled and sat down next to Rochelle.

"So Nic, how have you been?" Rochelle held my hands. "I want to know everything! Last time I saw you, you had a boyfriend didn't you. What was his name again?"

"Oh Ricky, yeh that ended a long time ago, I think it was August of 99'. He was a knob, but oh well. Other than that, I've been really busy actually: I passed all my exams at the end of college, and then I also got a job at the leisure centre, but I left that to come here."

"That's great to hear Nic, I'm so happy you're coming to work for us. We've been looking for a receptionist for ages. We were thinking you could work four days a week - Monday and Wednesday in Crystal Palace, and then Tuesday and Thursday in Beckenham?" She looked at me. "Is that alright lovely?"

"Yes, that sounds perfect." I smiled- deep down, I was very happy that she had got the memo that I don't like to work Fridays that much. I laughed to myself at that.

"You can come out with me on Fridays." Romeo piped up. I suddenly got flustered, and didn't know what to say, but something inside of me stepped up and replied "Of course, sounds great!"

Drinks started flowing- Romeo definitely had more than he should've done. I was drinking more than I usually do - which was definitely a mistake. Rochelle was downing shots on the kitchen side and stumbling about. She didn't know what to do with herself, and if I'm honest neither did I... my head was so foggy, I didn't really know what I was doing, or where I was.

I think the time was about 1am by this point, and I was sprawled on their grey sofa, with Romeo next to me. He was barely awake, but I think he was sobering up.

"You look really nice today, Nikki." That just proved he was drunk; how could he find me attractive? I couldn't believe what I was hearing.

"You're too drunk- we should take you up to bed."

"Ok, but can you stay with me for a bit once we get upstairs."

"Fine." I rolled my eyes- I was too drunk to care to be honest.

We both stumbled up the stairs towards the top floor, making more noise than if an elephant had trundled up.

When we got into the room, we both collapsed onto his bed.

5

My eyes began to slowly open, although it took a while for me to adjust. I couldn't really see anything - all I could feel was this huge headache throbbing and throbbing. It was almost blocking my vision in a weird way. I had no real recollection of what had happened last night- my mind was a complete blank canvas. My eyes opened properly and then I realised that this wasn't my room. "Oh my god. Oh my god. Oh my god." I panicked - I turned around to see Romeo snoring next to me. I knew I had to act quickly before he saw me.

I trod very lightly, trying to not make a sound. Luckily, the floors were not as squeaky as the ones that we had at home. I walked back into my room and went into my bed, pretending that nothing had ever happened. I lay staring at my wall overthinking about all of the possibilities until I just wanted to block it out of my brain.

Eventually. I plucked the courage to get up, get my clothes on and walk downstairs. I was greeted in the kitchen by a whole buffet of breakfast done by Rochelle.
"Rochelle, how is your head not hurting?" I stared in awe.
"You'll get used to it living in London- it's all part of the fun." She laughed to herself.
In my head I thought, should I tell her? Then I decided not to, and to just keep it a complete secret. I didn't want

anyone to know - I didn't even really know whatever had happened.

"Did you have a good sleep, Nikki?"

Oh no. How am I going to dodge this one?

"Er…yeah, it was good. How did you sleep?"

"Oh yeah fine, I'm surprised you slept well with all the traffic noise coming from the side your bedroom is on. That's why Romeo sleeps on the other side."

I looked down for a second and then looked up. I took a deep breath,

"Yeah, it didn't bother me at all. The room is so lovely - thank you so much for being so generous."

"It's my pleasure, we're so happy you're here. And I'm so glad you can keep Romeo company - you two seem to be getting on quite well." She grinned.

"He's a laugh - I really like him." I was trying not to let slip what had happened - I was so embarrassed and prayed it wasn't showing in my face.

"Well, he seems happy you're here. I think he gets quite lonely sometimes." She looked at me seriously. "He used to live with his wife up in Newcastle, but their marriage ended quite publicly in 1999. They had two children together, but she moved away to America after the divorce."

What did she just say? Romeo has two children? He's been divorced? I couldn't believe what I was hearing. I gasped.

"Oh my… I never knew. How old are the kids?"

"The oldest one is three and then the youngest one is nine months."
"How does he see them if she's just ditched to go to America?"
"He doesn't - you can tell it kills him. Sometimes he doesn't come out of his room all day. He just lies there. But I think you coming to stay has brought something out of him that I haven't seen in ages."

Secretly, I was so happy she had said that. I didn't want to show much emotion though.
"That's so nice, he's been so good to me ever since I got here."
"I'm glad." Rochelle swiftly left the room and walked towards the stairs. "Andre, Romeo - breakfast!" She screamed. I heard loud footsteps above me. Within seconds, both of them were downstairs sitting at the table. Rochelle placed their plates at either end, so they were facing each other. I sat next to Romeo, she sat next to Andre, and we all started eating. I have never seen anyone eat as quickly as Romeo did - he had managed to leave no crumbs - his plate was spotless.

"Nic, I'm going to show you around London today if that's alright. The boys are going to watch the football down the road at Selhurst Park." Rochelle offered.
I looked up and smiled. "Of course, that sounds great. What time do you want to leave?"

"We'll leave in about an hour - I can show you all the sights!"

"Can't wait!"

"What time will you guys be back?" Andre asked.

"Early-evening. Maybe six or seven? Then we can all eat together."

"That sounds good. Shall I book a restaurant - saves us getting pissed in our living room for the second night in a row!" She giggled.

Back upstairs, I packed my bag full of anything I might need - mints, spray, wipes, my wallet and my phone. I changed into a white crop top, white trousers with a denim jacket. I didn't really care if I was cold because I'd rather look fashionable (controversial I know, but that's how my priorities work). I ran downstairs where Rochelle was by the door.

"I don't have any good shoes to wear, oh my god." I said to her, panicking,

"What size are you?"

"5.5."

"Twins! You can borrow these boots."

I was shocked. They were the kind of boots you saw in All-Saints - unlike the ones I had at home that were from the pound shop.

"Are you sure?"

"Of course, take them!"

I pulled them on, Rochelle opened the door and we walked towards the station.

When we got to the station, Rochelle bought us a ticket each which was called a Travelcard - I had never heard of it.

"They allow you to go anywhere in London for a whole day. I used to get these all the time and explore different places with it. It was such a fun thing to do!"

"Does that mean we can ride any train we want?"

"Absolutely!"

I followed Rochelle through the barriers towards the platform and we boarded the train back up to Victoria.

Although it was only a day since I was back in Victoria on my way to Rochelle's, it felt longer. Like, a lot longer.

"First, I'm going to show you Buckingham Palace - where the queen lives!"

"Is that near?"

"Yes, like five minutes away." She replied, ushering me out of the station and up the road.

I looked above my head at the skyscrapers towering above me - I didn't understand how buildings could be built so high. They were so tall they shadowed the sky- but beautiful at the same time. We walked up a street, and right in front of my eyes was Buckingham Palace. I had never seen it in real life before and, to be honest, I was a bit let down - it wasn't as magical as I thought it was going to be.

Rochelle got her camera out. Oh god, I thought, I did not like getting my picture taken. At all. "Let's get a picture of you outside the gates of Buckingham Palace."
I stood by the gates, did a pose and then we moved on quite quickly.
"This strip is called The Mall; it leads up to Trafalgar Square. It's very historical - but I can't remember why." Rochelle explained. By this point it had started raining, and Rochelle put up her hood over her wavy brown hair. I had no hood, but it didn't really bother me as I was used to the rain down in Brighton.
"It's very pretty." I pointed at all of the trees. "And very green, I didn't realise London had so much greenery."
"It's gorgeous, I love living here. I much prefer it to living down by the sea in Worthing." Rochelle stated. "Let's get a coffee when we get to Trafalgar Square, and we'll have a girl's catch up shall we?"
"Sounds great!" I replied - but inside I started to panic as I didn't want her to ask me about Romeo or whether I had feelings for him. I was still reeling from finding out he had two children already.

We walked up into a cafe, and Rochelle ordered us a latte each. We sat down on a brown sofa in the corner. I took a sip out of my coffee, but it burnt my tongue, so I put it back down.
"So, Rochelle, what's been going on at home. Any drama to catch me up on?"

"Not really, I think the last real drama was when Steph broke off her engagement four days before the wedding." Steph was our cousin, she was a year older than me, so four years younger than Rochelle. She had originally been planning to get married in November of 1999 but called it off- itt was a proper family scandal.

"I remember that; I was supposed to come down to Hove the day after to get ready for the wedding at my parents' house. That was horrible of Steph. I remember how heartbroken Declan was after he found out- poor boy." Rochelle said, and I nodded in agreement. "What is Steph doing now?" She asked.

"God knows- last I heard she had moved to Benidorm to work as a travel agent, but I saw her down in the Churchill shopping centre in Brighton a few months ago. She completely blanked me- walked straight past like she hadn't even seen me."

"That's odd. That girl can be so rude sometimes." Rochelle didn't look very happy. "Anyway, I would never invite her to come and stay with me."

"Haha, I wouldn't either if I had a house."

"At least I went through with my wedding- she couldn't even do that."

"Did you ever get cold feet before your wedding?" I wondered out loud.

"Of course - who doesn't? But I knew he was the right man in the end. Although, I had been engaged before Andre."

I was shocked: "Wait… how did I never know this?" I asked in confusion.

"I was probably about your age when it happened- I had moved to Manchester. Remember that?"

"Oh yeah, I didn't realise it was for a guy though?"

"He moved there, and I decided to follow him- it was so stupid looking back now. He was the same age as Romeo - 25. I wish I had never moved up there. Biggest mistake ever, because he turned out to be cheating on me."

"Oh, Roch, that's horrible- I'm so sorry."

"You don't have to be - it doesn't matter anymore, because I've got Andre. I met him after it all went wrong, and we got married in 1998 - well, eloped. And then, the new salon came in 1999. So, life got better and now here we are in 2000. You're going to be nineteen in a few weeks and I'm going to be twenty-four in June. That's crazy!"

"God, I don't want another year to pass quickly." I looked at Rochelle who tilted her head in agreement.

"I'm just going to retouch my makeup, and then we'll go see the next sight!"

"Ok, I'll just wait here for you." I replied. Rochelle turned and walked to the toilet. I reached for my phone out of my bag and quickly checked it - I had a few messages, one from my dad.

Hey, Nic. Miss you loads already, hope you're having a great time. Dad x

I quickly messaged him back.

Hey dad, miss you too. Everything is going great thanks! I will come and visit you in a few weeks xx

Rochelle walked out of the toilet. I stood up and followed her out of the door of the Cafe.

"I'm going to show you Piccadilly Circus now!" She exclaimed as we walked side by side.

"That sounds exciting - I think I've heard of it before. Is that where all the big billboards are?"

"Yes! It is."

As we strolled up the street, I could see all the big red double decker buses that I had seen in films. It really did feel like I was in a movie! But I'd never seen anything so busy in my life- even Brighton beach on a hot afternoon in the summer had nothing on this!

When we got to the centre of Piccadilly circus, I could see just how busy it was. People were rushing around at a million miles an hour- I had never seen anything like it in my life! It was a Saturday, but there were still lots of people dressed like construction workers, while it was also teeming with families. Rochelle got the camera out again.

"Nikki, let's get another photo!"

So, again I posed in front of Piccadilly Circus, and she snapped with her camera- I felt like I was being papped! It was quite fun though; I did enjoy it. Swiftly, we moved onto Leicester Square.

"I'm really enjoying myself Rochelle - thanks so much for taking me out!"

"It's my pleasure- I love showing people around my city."

"Where are we now?" I could see these red decorative flags all around.

"This is Chinatown, just on the way to Leicester Square." She explained. "I come here whenever Andre and I want to see a film in the cinema."

"That's so cool- I guess this is all just a few minutes on the train from you?"

"Yes - and now you!" She giggled and then smiled at me kindly.

We continued to walk through London and then through to the shops in Covent Garden.

"This place is so pretty."

"This is Covent Garden market. It's a bit overpriced, but it can be worth it sometimes."

"This ring is so pretty." I said, admiring it on my finger. Within a split second, Rochelle yanked it off. "You have to ask before you try it on or we'll get in trouble!" I think she saw the funny side of it though, because she was laughing really hard.

She swiftly moved us away from that stall and onto the next. I really liked all the stuff I saw, but the price tags were making me feel sick. Rochelle was going to be paying me more money than a normal receptionist would usually get, but even so these price tags were completely out of my budget.

By the time we had done all this window shopping and walking, it was already about four in the afternoon.

"Shall we get back to the house to get some dinner?"

"Yes, I'm quite tired all of a sudden."

"Haha- London does that to you a lot actually!"

We got back to the house and Rochelle opened the door. I felt like collapsing, I was so tired from all that walking. It had been a really good day though, and I think I was starting to fall in love with London. I went back upstairs and laid on my bed for a few moments before having a shower and changing into a red dress for dinner. The dress was quite tight, as it was only a size four, but it fit well enough. The boys were still not back from football, so I quickly went downstairs to get a second opinion on the dress from Rochelle.

"Oh Nikki, I love it. I actually love it! It suits you so well."

Just as I was walking back towards the stairs, Andre and Romeo walked through the door.

"We're back!" Andre shouted. "Hey Nic, did you have a good day?"

"Yes, it was really good." I don't even think Andre took any notice of the dress but that was good.

"You look stunning Nikki." Romeo announced. He then gave me a kiss on the cheek.

I stood there stunned for a second. I had no idea why he was kissing me on the cheek. Did he know something I didn't?

6

It was Monday morning, my first day working at the salon. I was really nervous about starting, because it was a new job, in a completely new place, with completely new people. I looked over at the clock on my bedside table: 8:02am. I didn't want to get out of bed though, because I felt really sick - I think it was nerves, but I could barely move. Finally, I plucked the courage to push away my duvet and got out of bed. I woke up to Rochelle having laid out my uniform by the bottom of my bed. I quickly put it on and rushed downstairs. I still felt really sick.

"Nikki, are you ready to go?" Andre shouted across the house to me.
"Yes, I'm just about ready. Shall I get my shoes on?"
"Not yet, come and have some breakfast." Rochelle said.
I walked into the kitchen, and she handed me a Blueberry muffin on a plate.
"Here you go, Nic. These are so so good!"
"Thank you so much."
I sat down on a chair and quickly devoured the muffin, meanwhile Andre was rushing around trying to get everything sorted. While this was all happening, Romeo was lying upstairs asleep. I was kind of wishing I was asleep and not feeling this sickness in the pit of my stomach.

We left the house; Andre locked the door. We walked up to the high street where the salon was. At this point it was pretty much empty, as it was not even 9am- I could barely see anyone. We walked up to this all-white chic salon, called Salon 222. I was unsure of the name, but the rest of it was very glamorous.

Rochelle put an ornate looking key into the door and opened up. In front of us was a waiting space filled with pink benches, a pink desk with a sign saying 'check-in' and above the desk, a large painting with the Salon 222 logo on it.

"Come upstairs Nikki, we'll go into the staff room."

The stairs were quite steep and there were quite a few of them. Rochelle pushed open a door at the top of the stairs where we entered a room. This room looked like it had been left when they were doing the renovations. It was quite dingy, but I wasn't going to say anything about it.

"Would you like a coffee? Or tea?" Rochelle asked.

"Can I get some water please?"

"Of course."

I was just desperate to get something that would get rid of this sickness feeling in my body. It was wearing me down completely, but I didn't want Rochelle or Andre to know. It was my first day of work - how embarrassing would it have been to have to go back home on my first day because I felt sick?

Rochelle passed me a glass of water and I gulped it down. We then both walked downstairs to the front desk, where there was a phone and a list of the appointments for the week.

"So, what you've got to do is check-in the clients as they come in. They'll be given a chair number, so send them where they need to go." Rochelle pointed at the back door. "Our hairdressers and aesthetic workers will come in through that door."

"Ok thank you!"

"Just enjoy yourself- you will love it!" Rochelle smiled at me.

As the day went on, I felt less and less sick - so I knew it must have been down to nerves. The job itself was quite easy and all the customers were really nice and welcoming. I ticked away as people walked in, and I didn't have to clean anything except hair, which I was grateful for. You never know what would be waiting for you to clean at the leisure centre…

By the time it was 6pm, the sun had set, and it was dark outside. The last customer walked out of the salon, and it was time to relax.

"You did such a good job today Nikki- I'm so proud of you." Rochelle gave me (quite a tight) hug.

"Thanks Roch, I love your salon! I can't wait to come back tomorrow."

"We will take you to the other one tomorrow, which is where Andre mainly works - so he'll show you the ropes."
"Perfect."
Rochelle shut all the doors and switched off all of the lights. She put the shutter over the shop, and we walked back to the house.

As soon as we got back, I ran upstairs and got changed. I lay on my bed, and sat and read a magazine. I heard a knock on the door. It made me jump- but I presumed it was Rochelle.
"Hello?"
Romeo walked in.
"Hey." I said softly.
"Hey, I'm bored. Can I come in?"
"Sure, come sit." I pointed at the other side of the bed. He sat down.

Then without evening thinking I blurted:
"I like you."

Why did I do that? I immediately felt myself going red in the face. I was mortified. I had no idea why I just said that. But his response shocked me more:
"So do I."

I gasped. Hopefully internally, but I can't imagine it was. "I have liked you ever since I first saw you. Your long blonde hair, your figure, your eyes." He looked at me.

"Oh my god, I wasn't expecting you to respond like that."

"What did you think I was going to say?"

"I thought you would not have liked me back. First of all, you're twenty-five!"

"And what?" He replied.

"You've got two kids!" I blurted out.

I thought this might upset him, but he took it surprisingly well.

"I get your points, but I still really like you. I would love it if you would come out on a date with me- maybe then we can actually get to know each other?"

"I'd love that."

"I'll take you out on Friday when you have a day off, how about that?"

"I'll be there!" I replied, beaming.

Four days later, it was Thursday. The last day of my working week. The date was 24th February. Tomorrow was my date with Romeo. I woke up as normal, but the sickness I had on Monday had returned, and this time was in full force. I could barely lift my head up off the pillow. I did eventually have to get out of bed, and I rushed down to the toilet where I lay next to the bowl for about thirty minutes. I wasn't actually sick, so I decided to pretend nothing had happened and got back to getting ready for work. Again, as the day progressed, the sickness got better, and had basically disappeared by the end of the day. It left me completely puzzled; I had no idea what was going on. Why was I always sick?

7

My eyes opened slowly, I felt sick again. Ugh, this was the third day this week. But this time it was much, much, much worse than it had ever felt. I felt like I was carrying the weight of the world on my shoulders. I couldn't move, I was frozen. I lay in my bed staring at the ceiling - wondering how I was supposed to get out of bed for my date with Romeo. I had no idea what I looked like, but I imagined it wasn't my best.

Eventually, I got out of bed and walked over to the bathroom. Suddenly, all my limbs felt like they had shut down and I collapsed down to the floor. I managed to open the toilet bowl up just in time for all the vomit to come spewing out. I quickly flushed the chain and shut the door of the bathroom, making sure there was not even a sign that I had ever been in there.

Throwing up was all I needed, I felt so much better after it. I was able to go back upstairs and get ready. Nobody needed to know I threw up in the toilet - although I was slightly worried as to what was causing this constant nausea. I was hoping I had cleared it- it was the only thing bringing me down at the moment.

I put on my makeup and my leather jacket and black crop top and walked downstairs. The house was empty -

Rochelle and Andre must have already left. Romeo quickly followed me down the stairs and met me in the kitchen.

"You alright, Nikki? You look gorgeous today."

"Thank you, that's very kind." I could feel myself going red with a combination of both excitement and embarrassment.

"I am so excited for our day out together today; I've pulled some strings and I've booked a really posh restaurant in Mayfair for lunch."

"How? Should I go and change? I'm a bit underdressed, aren't I?"

"Don't worry about it - I'm only going to wear a red tracksuit that I got from my club."

"Ok cool, what time do you want to leave?"

"The taxi will be here in half an hour."

"The taxi? Are we not going by train?"

"Not with me we don't."

I was confused. I knew he was a footballer, but I didn't think footballers were that glamorous- and he wasn't exactly world class. After all, he had only just got his cast off his broken arm and now had a bandage.

I could hear a car screech up outside the front door. I poked my head outside of the top floor window to have a look, and there parked on the pavement was a luxury 4x4 with blacked out windows. My mind just couldn't keep up- less than a week ago I had never left the South Coast! This was crazy, I couldn't believe it - I thought I was seeing things until Romeo shouted upstairs "It's here, It's here. Quick Nic, we need to go."

As I walked towards the car, a driver got out and came around to the side of the car facing the house and pulled open the door. The driver was dressed in an all-black suit and had slicked back hair. He smiled at me, and I smiled at him - but behind me Romeo handed the driver two £50 notes. I was shocked- my jaw dropped to what felt like the floor. I had never seen a £50 note in my life! I was genuinely baffled. How much money did Romeo have? What else was he hiding? In the week I had known him (well under a week) I had found out he was a footballer, that he had two children who lived in America, and now I find out he is actually really, really rich.

The driver shut the doors for us, and then got back into the driver's seat. He quickly drove off the pavement and back onto the roads.

"How come you have £50 notes Romeo? I've never seen them in my life."

"You've never seen them, how?" He pulled out his wallet, filled with £50 notes. My jaw dropped again. By this point, my mouth was aching from all the shocks.

"Where do you get all this money from?"

Well, he didn't hide it. "I'm on a £30,000 a week contract at my club."

Sorry what? £30k! I don't think I will earn that in five

years. I was too stunned to speak. For what must have been the first time in my life, I was speechless.

"Your life is crazy. So why did you come down here to stay at your brother's house in South East London?"
"Because I was written off training for six weeks- and sometimes I just have to escape. But I do have to go back on 7th March."
"Do you still get paid even when you're injured?" I enquired.
"Yep, that's football. They are losing a lot of money because of my salary. I'm the second highest earner in the whole club - third highest in my division."
"No need to brag." I laughed.
"Haha, sorry it's not my intention, it's just the truth."

We pulled up on a large street in Mayfair, it reminded me of the buildings that I saw when Rochelle took me around London on my second day here. It was very posh, people on either side were dressed in evening gowns or suits. I unwinded the window to look out, and saw a restaurant painted all red, with two men standing outside wearing waistcoats with decorative patterns. The driver leapt out of his seat and opened the door for us.
"Here you go." He leant out his hand to help me get out. As I got out, I noticed a flash in my eyes - I didn't see any sign of where it was coming from, so I just ignored it. We walked into the restaurant. The first thing I noticed was how luxurious it looked - the walls were gold, and there

was a dragon mural on the ceiling. I don't think I have ever seen anything like it - and I know that I have definitely never ever eaten in a restaurant like it.

We sat down at a table near the back, and the waitress put a menu on either side of the table. I took one look at the menu and blurted out "What is all this posh crap? I don't understand what it says."
Romeo obviously looked quite embarrassed, as we looked like slobs compared to the rest of the people sitting in this restaurant.
"You can't say that Nikki, they might kick us out." By this point, his cheeks were flushed red. I felt quite bad, but sometimes I just can't control my mouth, so I didn't feel as guilty as I maybe should've done. I just needed this date to get back on track as quickly as possible.

"So- why didn't you need this much security when you went out to watch the football with your brother?"
"I just didn't."
He seemed quite defensive by this point and the date seemed like it was going south quite quickly; how was I going to turn this around?

He broke the silence. "What else are you planning on doing while you're living in London?"
"I'd love to try the nightlife- as much as Brighton nightlife is fun, there's only so many times you can end up lying drunk on the beach and falling asleep."

"What!? You slept on the beach?"

"Yeah, a few times actually- when I turned seventeen, we went out partying with fake IDs and ended up on the beach."

"What did your parents think?" He asked.

"Well, it was only my dad- and he was very angry when I got home the next morning at 8:30am."

"Oh ok, where was your mum?"

"She moved away when I was seven. I haven't seen her since."

"Oh, that's so sad- I'm so sorry Nikki."

"It's fine, don't worry about it." I replied. I was not bothered that he asked me considering how I had embarrassed him just minutes earlier.

When the waitress came, I got Romeo to order a steak for me, and he got the same but even he struggled to pronounce what they had written on the menu. The menus said the steaks were £90 each- what a rip off - I thought to myself. I was waiting to see whether it was worth the hefty price tag, but I was pretty certain it wasn't going to beat a steak from down the local pub back home.

Even though the date had gotten off to a really poor start, I was liking Romeo more and more. I found his arrogance somewhat attractive, and he was quite charming and kind. The steaks arrived quite quickly, and we both tucked in. "Oh my god, it's so good." I said in pure joy. Although, still not worth £39 in my mind.

"Yeah, I agree, these are the best steaks in London I think." He looked at me seriously. "I used to come here with my ex all the time when we were dating."

"Did you live down here?" I asked, interested to hear the backstory between Romeo and his ex.

"It was 1995- I played at a club in West London, and we lived just a 20-minute tube ride from here. Before I used to get noticed, life was easy."

I have got to be honest, I thought Romeo was being quite dramatic, because his life wasn't exactly hard; he had money, a great job, he had a good life - except for the fact he couldn't see his kids.

"I was thirteen in 1995. That's so crazy." I laughed to myself.

As he swallowed down a bite of his steak. He started speaking again, "Me and my ex - her name was Chloe. We were together for the best part of four years. She was in the industry just like I was."

"She was a footballer?" I was confused.

"No, she was in the music industry originally, in a girl group, but afterwards we were just a famous couple."

"If it makes you feel any better, I didn't know who you were." I retracted. "Sorry, that was unhelpful. I shouldn't have said that."

"No, don't worry, the ordeal was quite traumatic for both of us. Our every move was monitored in the public eye. I think she really struggled because in a band, the focus was never on her, but now it was."

"What kind of things were written about you?"

"I had one story which said I had cheated on her, another said she slapped me round the face. There was one where it was a four-page spread of a fight we had on our honeymoon in Cape Verde."

"Was it all untrue?"

"Yeah, most of it. Except Chloe's cocaine binge that hit the press early last year. I think that's what tore us apart."

"Oh wow." I was stunned- I didn't know how to respond.

"Yeah, sorry I got a bit deep then. This was supposed to be a fun date."

"It's fine. Let's talk about other stuff. I've got a question: what made you want to be a footballer?"

"Well, my dad used to play football before he and my mum set up the business, but he got me and Andre playing from a young age."

"How young were you?" I wasn't actually interested but I was trying to swerve from sore subjects like the breakdown of his marriage - or his druggie ex-wife.

"I was six, Andre must have been about three. Andre was better than I was at that age, but he quit when he got injured. I carried on and my dad moved to Southampton so we could live where I was training. I signed my first pro contract when I was fourteen."

"That's so young. My ex is a footballer- although not a very good one. He still lives with his parents."

"Being a footballer is harder than it seems- I know you probably have your preconceived ideas of what footballers are like, but we're not just lazy and greedy. Well, at least not all of us. Anyway, what's your dream? I can't imagine you want to be a receptionist forever, do you?"

"No of course not- but it's definitely good for now. I really wanted to be a glamour model, but I don't know if that is a good idea at the minute."

"Why not? I think you would make a great glamour model." He smiled at me. "I can get you in touch with my PR and my management. If they think you're good enough, they'll get you in for a couple of shoots and see what happens."

I was speechless. I know I've never mentioned this, but I have always wanted to be a glamour model. When I was younger, I was always being scouted out to do shoots, but my dad would never let me because he wanted me to stay in school, and I needed parental consent. So, there were never any modelling shoots for me.

"That would be amazing, I would love that. But my focus is on the salon, as I said to Rochelle that's what I would do while I'm out here."

"I get that - but also, she would understand." He smiled. He reached for his pocket and pulled out his Motorola, and quickly dialled up a number. I could hear the phone ringing from across the table. I could only make out what Romeo was saying on his end and who the other one was.

'Hi Keira, do you know of any managers who represent glamour models - I think I know someone who would be great in the industry and really wants to do it'

'Ok cool, I'll ring that number later. Thank you so much Keira.'

He put his phone back in his pocket. "I've got the number of someone we can call to get you in the industry. Now, you don't have to do it, but the option is always going to be there, whether or not you want to take it."
My brain was going a million miles an hour- I didn't realise he would be so quick to decide and do all that for me.
"Ok, I'll think about it. Thank you though. I appreciate it." I smiled and he smiled back. By this point, the waitress had come over to give the bill. Romeo swiftly paid and left a hefty tip (£100). I couldn't get over all this constant throwing money around.

Romeo got up and so I followed. "Thank you." The waitress said. "Thank you so much, it was so good." I replied. Romeo pushed the door open for me and said, "Ladies first." I thought that was really cute. "Thank you."

"Let's go for a walk. The taxi will be here in a few minutes."
"Ok cool. I'd like that."

We walked up the street for a couple of minutes and talked. By this point, we were holding hands. I could feel butterflies at the pit of my stomach - I was just glad it wasn't vomit to be honest. Suddenly, out of nowhere Romeo turns to me and says, "Can I kiss you?"
I was a bit confused, and I didn't really know what to do. I wanted to kiss him too but it was all so unexpected.
"Ok… sure."
He kissed me, but as I went in, a flash crossed my eyes and almost blinded me.

SNAP.

8

My eyes opened wide. It was Saturday morning. I had no idea what I was going to do today- I was hoping it was just going to be a chill day. I hadn't had one the whole time I had been in London - although it had only been eight days. I was really enjoying my time here, and although yesterday had been a borderline date disaster, I was excited to continue getting to know Romeo. I didn't come here to find a man, but I was going to continue to learn more about him.

I couldn't get the kiss out of my head though: why was there a flash as soon as it happened? It must have just been in my head- but I had no idea why. I was stressed about all of that, plus I felt sick again. Ugh, how annoying - I was over it by this point. It had been continuous all week, but I was still determined not to throw up.

I heard a knock on my door. "Come in." I said.
"Hey Nic, You alright? The boys have gone to watch football again today. What would you like to do?"
"I'm alright, I'm down for whatever." I replied shyly.
"You look quite sheepish, are you alright?"
I thought this was the right point to come clean- I didn't want to hide it any longer.
"Most mornings this week, I've woken up feeling quite sick. It's been horrific."

"Aw, babe you should have told me. I would have sorted you out." She looked concerned. "Tell you what, we'll go down to the shops, and go get some chocolate and booze from the off-licence."

"Ok sounds great. Thank you, it's really sweet of you." I smiled back, trying to withhold everything from coming out.

"Ready to go?" Rochelle shouted up to me.

"One minute!" I replied back.

"Of course, take your time."

I ran down the stairs, and we were out of the door. Rochelle was a quick walker so I struggled to keep up with her at the best of times, but at this point I was just walking at my own pace. The corner shop was only a two-minute walk away.

When we got to the corner shop, it was quite small, and we were immediately greeted with a really tough door that I had to use all my strength to push open. Rochelle walked in through first and I immediately noticed a panicked look on her face.

"What's wrong?" I asked.

"N-nothing. Don't worry. Just head straight for the sweet aisle.

I walked in, but immediately clocked the newspaper rack. They all had the same photo.

'Romeo Lomax kisses new girlfriend!'

'Romeo Lomax kisses 18-year-old!'

'Footballer Romeo Lomax seen kissing unknown blonde with striking similarities to ex Chloe King...'

I gasped. Rochelle rushed to console me, but it was too late. My legs, my arms, even my face started to feel numb, and I felt myself collapse to the floor. I was drifting into unconsciousness, but I could make out some of what was going on around me.

"Get an ambulance, get an ambulance." Rochelle shrieked. "A woman has collapsed in my shop, please get an ambulance here soon."
"She is still breathing, what should we do?"
"Ok thank you."

My eyes started to reopen just moments later; I could feel someone clutching my hand - it was Rochelle. I still could barely process what was happening -I felt so dazed and sick. My vision was blurry, I was barely hearing things, and I couldn't get up.

"Nicola, Nicola, Nicola, Nicola, Are you alright?"
I attempted to respond but I couldn't even move my lips apart, so I just moved my head up and down. I could just about make out Rochelle's traumatised face and the shop owner lent by my other side. My hair was covering my left

eye so I could barely see, but I knew he had caught on after he looked at the newspaper rack.

Within minutes, the paramedics swooped in, and I was led away on a stretcher. Rochelle was still clutching onto me as she got into the back of the ambulance. My eyes were wide open at this point, and my hearing had come back.

"Do you know what's wrong with her?" Rochelle asked the paramedic.
"I think she passed out due stress, or shock." She replied.
"Do you think anything could have led her to collapsing?"
"Well, she had just seen her face on the front of every national newspaper."
"What?" The paramedic looked stunned.
"It's a long story- but I just hope she's ok."
"She will be just fine, I promise you."

I was wheeled out of the ambulance and into the hospital. I still didn't really know what was going on- my mind felt like it was being blurred by a big grey cloud. They transferred me over to a hospital bed where I was put on a drip. Rochelle was sitting on a chair beside me.
"Nicola, it's all going to be alright. They're going to run a few tests on you to see what's going on."
I could finally move my lips and I mouthed the words "ok."

A doctor walked in, he ran the tests on me - I didn't really know much of what was going on- and then he left. He said he would be back when he had the results.

"Nic, I'm going to leave for a second. I need to phone Andre." She said, I nodded as a reply. "I'll be back." Rochelle rushed towards the door, leaving it ajar behind her so I could just about work out what she was saying. *'Nicola collapsed in the newsagents, she's not very well. She saw herself on the front of every national newspaper and she was gone.'*
'Why is she on the front of the newspapers? I thought Romeo had made sure that no photographers would be around. I'm angry, Andre. The girl is eighteen years old; she should not have to be the subject of a media firestorm. No, I don't trust your brother at all, this can't be good for her. I don't care if he can hear you. We will sort this out when we get home later."

Rochelle rushed back into the room, and I pretended as if I hadn't heard anything. Just seconds later, the same doctor who had taken the tests came back in.

"Well, you might want to sit down for this one. It might come as quite a shock to both of you." He explained.
"Go on, what is it?" Rochelle asked.
"Nicola is pregnant."
I was in a state of shock. "What? How can I be pregnant." I whispered in disbelief.

"You're about sixteen weeks along." He said.
"She's sixteen weeks, how? She's tiny."
"We think she's sixteen weeks anyway- as a minimum."

My body couldn't take all these shocks at once, I felt it shut down again. Everything went numb. How could I go from being a normal girl, to being on the front page of the news, and now pregnant, all in one day? I was startled, confused, shocked, and totally mortified. I knew who the father of the child was immediately- it had to be my ex-boyfriend Ricky. Why this? Why now? I was going to have to move back to Brighton and live with my dad. I couldn't raise a child on my own, I was pretty much still a child myself.
Pregnant. I couldn't believe it.

9

I woke up in a really uncomfortable bed. I didn't know where I was for a split second, but then remembered I was in the hospital. I could see a blue curtain wrapped around the section of the ward I had. I was still in shock as I lay thinking about the fact I was pregnant. I was only eighteen- I didn't need this. I was going to have to go back home, I couldn't stay with Rochelle anymore- it wouldn't be fair. She wouldn't want a baby walking around her house wrecking her pristine walls and perfect furniture.

I wondered what had really happened and cast my mind back to Saturday. All I could really remember was that I was on the front page of every national newspaper in the entire country. I couldn't believe that either. It must have been when I kept seeing all the flashes, because I vividly remember the headline being accompanied by a shot of me and Romeo kissing. Why was there a camera there? Why did Romeo want to kiss me at that exact point?

As this was all going through my head, Rochelle walked in with Andre and Romeo.
"You alright Nic?"
"Yeah, I think so. I feel much better today."
"The doctor says they're going to discharge you today."
"Thank god."
"I can't believe you're pregnant." Romeo piped up.

"I don't know how or why, but I definitely didn't need this now." I looked at Rochelle. "I'll have to move back to Brighton- I can't live with you if I have a baby."

"Don't be silly." Rochelle tried to reassure me. "We will all help you look after this baby."

I debated whether to ask Romeo about the newspaper articles, knowing what I had heard when Rochelle and Andre had been on the phone to each other.

"They now think you're about eighteen weeks along." Rochelle explained.

"Oh wow, how did I not notice? That must have been why I was feeling so sick all week. Did I collapse because I was pregnant?"

"No, you collapsed because you went into a state of shock. I think it was seeing your face on the news. Your blood pressure completely dropped."

Andre quickly chimed in. "Romeo and I are going to go back to the house to sort everything out. We'll catch you later."

They walked out, waving at me, and pushed the curtain away to get out.

"Right, I'll explain to you." Rochelle looked at me sternly.

"Explain to me what?" I looked confused.

"Why you're on the front page of every national newspaper in the UK."

Oh no. What is she going to say? I don't know if I want to know. My heart was racing.

"Go for it, why?"

"Well, what Romeo did - which we told him explicitly not to do- is tip off the media and the paparazzi and sold the rights to the pictures."

"What?" I couldn't believe it. After he opened up about the media intrusion he had faced for years. Maybe he was in the wrong career - he was a great actor.

"How much did he sell them for? Surely I'm entitled to some of the money?"

"That's what we said. He wouldn't disclose how much he made- but we're kicking him out tomorrow morning if he doesn't give you your half."

My mind was blown. How could you sell pictures of yourself? You must have to be properly desperate.

"What does he need the money for? He makes £30,000 a week."

"I know it's insane - I think he's got an addiction to making money."

I was stunned. I felt completely betrayed. How could he do this to me? He just used me for extra cash. I was furious- all this stress wasn't good for me.

"Roch, I've been completely betrayed. What do I do now? This can't keep happening to me. In just over forty-eight hours, I was on the front of the national newspaper, found out I'm pregnant and now that the man I liked betrayed me."

"I know, it's awful. This is not what we expected to happen in your first two weeks of being in London. You're stronger than you know, I promise." She held my hand. "I'll be there for you every step of the way."

"Thanks Rochelle- you're the best. Does my dad know yet?"

"No. Are you going to tell him?"

I thought for a second, wondering what dad would say.

"I'll ring him later." I knew deep down; he would be either upset or disappointed in me. Or both.

"Take your time to process everything, I'll write you off work for the rest of the week, if that's alright? I think it's best for you to recover at home."

"Oh, thank you." I breathed a sigh of relief. I don't think I could have faced working with all this added stress I was under with the pregnancy.

"The papers will be trying to get in touch with you. That's why Romeo leaving is the best idea. We don't want the press to find out where you are, or where you live." She took a deep breath. "It might be better if you don't leave the house unless you're with someone or you're getting into a car."

"Ok I'll try my best to keep hidden."

"Stay strong for us Nic - I'll come pick you up later when the doctor says you're discharged."

"Thank you, Rochelle, for everything." A tear rolled down my cheek.

Rochelle left the room, and I was on my own again. What was next for my life? I'd come here for a new start, the beginning of my career. Now I was going to be a mum and I was practically homeless (I couldn't live with Rochelle and Andre forever - I know she offered, but it will be different when I have a baby).

I think I'll have to kiss goodbye to my potential glamour model career. I was going to have to put everything on hold - just for this baby. I needed money fast, and the only way to get that was to get a cut of the money Romeo had made. I needed it if I was going to raise this baby. I needed to find myself a small flat, I needed to buy toys and clothes and a cot and whatever else this baby might need.

At about 12pm, one of the nurses gave me a sandwich, and she sat with me and explained the next steps.
"You'll come back here for a checkup in two weeks, and you can find out the gender of the child from that scan."
"Ok, what should I be doing?"
"Take it easy, don't get yourself too stressed out, because we don't want you collapsing again."
What should I do with my life? It's over, I thought to myself. I wished none of this had ever happened- I just wanted my life back. These had been the most dramatic two weeks of my life. Well, that's actually not true…but I'll get onto that later. I felt for the nurse, because I can't

imagine I was the nicest patient, but can you blame me? I could barely process all of this.

By now, it was 3pm, and the doctor came in to see me.

"You can go home, but if there's any problems - however minor- you come straight back alright?"

"Of course, have you rung Rochelle?"

"Yes, she will be here any minute now."

I got up from out of the bed and followed the doctor to the front reception of the hospital. Rochelle ran up and gave me a hug.

"I'm so glad you're out0 come on, let's go." She said to me.

I followed her towards the car park. I hadn't been outside for about two days, so I presumed I looked like a vampire - coupled with the fact it was February so there was no way I'd be getting a tan.

"Wait for me." I said, trying to catch up with Rochelle. She was such a speed walker- it was actually annoying. We got into her grey Mini - which I would like to add was a new car- and she drove off.

"I bet you're glad to be leaving that place."

"Well, I have to go back there in two weeks. For the scan that tells me what gender it is." I explained.

"That's exciting- I wonder what it will be!"

"To be honest, I don't really care. I don't want this baby." I was over it, I was over it all. I was exhausted and had no time to be excited about what gender the baby was going to be. I wished I didn't have to think about it all.

"Nikki, don't say that. This is a great thing. You might not think that, but you're having a baby. Some people don't get to have the chance to have a baby. But I know you're young- I get that it's not ideal to be a mother at your age."

I understood where she was coming from, but then again it wasn't going to change my mind. I was so unhappy.

"What should I say to Romeo when I get back?"

"Try and get your half of the money, or even all of it. He's a prick."

"Do you not like him then?"

"No, I never have- he did the same to you as he did to his ex, the one after Chloe."

"There was one after Chloe?"

"Yes, her name was Pandora. She was just a bit older than you and they dated for three months at the end of last year. Until he sold pap shots of her for £100,000."

"£100,000?!"

"Yep, she was gutted Andre told me, but she got her revenge as she sold so many stories on him and got a gig on a TV show. She's got a book coming soon."

Wow. I thought to myself. Is that what I could do? I thought that was not my style though - revenge. I wasn't spiteful, but this was for my future child. I needed this money. I needed to find out who this Pandora was and how she did it all.

I needed revenge.

"Do you still know Pandora? I'd like her number."
"Why?" Rochelle looked confused.
"I want to know how she dealt with it, the media attention she received, you know."
"Er…yeah I think I do; I'll give it to you later."

Rochelle reversed onto the drive and parked up. I undid my seat belt and got out of the car quickly. Rochelle handed me the keys, and I opened the door.
"Hey Nic." Romeo tried to approach me.
"Don't speak to me." I walked straight past him, waved at Andre and walked up the stairs. Savage, I know, but I didn't care. I was mortified that I let someone like that in. He did me dirty. He sold me. I felt like I was nothing more than a bit of money. The stairs up to my room were a killer, they were hard on a normal day, but today they were extra hard.

I got upstairs and immediately grabbed my bag. I hadn't checked my phone in ages- I flipped it up to find a million messages, but that didn't bother me. All I needed to do was call my dad and tell him everything. I didn't know how it was going to go down though- he was an overreacter at the best of times. He was never violent, he just used to shut me out and not talk to me for a while. Our relationship has had its ups and downs, but I knew this news was not going to do it good.

I pressed the phone button, and it started ringing. My heart was pounding at a million miles an hour like I was going to have a heart attack. I couldn't stop. My phone kept ringing. No answer yet. Until.

'Hey Nikki, what's up?"

'Dad; are you sitting down?'

'No but I can.'

'Please sit down.

'Ok, I'm sitting. What is it mate?'

'I'm pregnant.'

'Not again.'

10

The year was 1997. It was summertime. I had just finished my GCSE exams. I was celebrating by the beach with my friends Alexandra, Bonnie and Bianca. Bianca was eighteen so she had bought us alcohol, and we were partying.

"I love watching the sunset on the beach." Bonnie said.
"Same." I replied. Although my eyes were slowly shutting - I had by this point downed a few too many spirit mixers. I was slurring and curled up on a blanket.

Alexandra and Bianca were below us watching the waves crash into the Brighton shoreline. I was at peace with my life. I had probably failed all my exams, but I was just happy to be in this moment with three of my best friends. It was such a nice moment. I remember falling asleep on the mat and sleeping there.

The next morning, I was woken up by Bianca at sunrise to watch it rise over the sea. As I got up, I felt a huge pain in my stomach. A pain I don't think I've ever felt before.
"Oh my god. I'm in so much pain. I don't know what to do." I clutched my stomach.
"What's the matter Nikki?" Bianca rushed to comfort me.
"My stomach- I have the worst cramps I've ever had."
"Sit down. Where is it hurting?"
I pointed to the centre of my stomach.

"Oh my god. You might be pregnant."

"What?"

"My friend Stacey had really bad cramps and we did a pregnancy test- and it was positive."

I froze on the spot. No way was I pregnant. I was sixteen years old. I didn't want a baby; I definitely didn't need a baby. My brother Carter had only been born two years before. How? I needed to get out of my own head. I was not going to be pregnant, I reassured myself.

"Once the other two have gone, we'll pop into town and get a test, and you can come back to mine and do it back at my place. My parents are away for the week in the villa in Spain."

"Thanks Bianca." I was breathing heavily by this point. I was so nervous. But it had to be done to rule it out. Although I did trust Bianca, I hoped this was all a complete lie- but she was deadly serious.

Once Alexandra and Bonnie had left, Bianca walked up to town holding my hand. All I could feel was sheer panic- I was so scared. Bianca bought the test and took me back to her house.

Bianca had this gorgeous house; it was a mock Tudor house and had a detached double garage to the side of it. It was one of the nicest houses I'd ever seen. We walked through the front door and Bianca marched me straight upstairs to her room. Well, when I say room, it was more multiple rooms. There was a walk-in wardrobe, and a bathroom conjoined to the main room. Bianca sat down on her bed, picked up a pair of scissors and ripped into the box. She pulled out the test from inside the box.

"Here you go." She passed it to me. "Go to the bathroom to do it."

I walked towards the bathroom and turned around to her and said, "I'm nervous."

"Don't be!" She replied.

I pushed open the door to the bathroom and locked it behind me. The bathroom was a confined space and it all made me extra nervous. I did everything that needed to be done for the test, followed every instruction on the box. And then stood there waiting for two minutes. I swear to God they were the worst two minutes of my life. My mind was racing, my heart was pounding. I was completely frozen, the limbs in my body were barely working. Everything felt stiff. I turned over the test after counting. Positive.

I gasped.

I couldn't move. Bianca was banging on the door, but I didn't want to say anything. Why did this happen to me? Why now? Everything was going right until now.

I felt scared, and so trapped. The bathroom walls felt like they were caving in on me. I had no idea what to do.

"Let me in, let me in! Nicola! Nikki!".

I still couldn't move. I tried to open my mouth, but it was clamped shut.

"Nikki?"

Bianca kept banging, but I didn't want to let her in. I was mortified. My body was shaking, my legs were numb. I felt as if I was going to collapse.

I stood there, ignoring the door. By this point, I had turned over the pregnancy test. It couldn't be true, how? I was only sixteen years old. I was due to start sixth form in only a few weeks- I couldn't go there if I was expecting a baby.

I slowly turned the key in the door and the door opened slightly. I fell into Bianca.

"Oh my god." Her eyebrows raised up to her hairline.

She held me tight and dragged me over to her bed. She put me down onto the sheets and I curled up into the side. Tears cascaded down both of my cheeks.

"Oh babe, we should get you to the hospital."

"I'm not going." I snapped back.

"You need to get a scan- we don't know how far along you are."

"Yes- but it's been ten minutes since I found out."

"Ok, fine"

I lay there, thinking to myself: my life will have to completely change.

"Why did I drink last night?" I said angrily.

"You can't beat yourself up about it- you didn't know."

I looked at Bianca and saw red. How could someone be so annoying? She was really getting on my nerves, and I was over her. She was really bugging me. She was my best friend most of the time, but today I couldn't bear her.

"I need to go." I said as I rushed out.

"Why? Your mascara is running down your face."

"Oh, please just leave me alone." I slammed the door and ran down the stairs. I slipped my shoes on and smashed the door behind me.

That was the last time I spoke to Bianca.

It was a regret I always had- that I never apologised. She moved up to Newcastle for university that September, and I never saw her again.

Bianca's street was endlessly long- it just kept going. I just needed to get on a bus to get back to Hove. I ran and I ran. My head was a mess, and it hurt. I was tripping over my shoes constantly. I was a wreck. I jumped on the first bus I could find, just because it would get me away from this place.

Thankfully, the bus dropped me off just two streets away from my house in Hove at Denmark Villas. I continued to run but I kept panting constantly- my whole body ached. My legs were constantly throbbing, and I could barely walk. My heart was beating really quickly - I couldn't work out whether it was from running, or from the fact I was going to tell my dad that I was pregnant. I knew he was going to be mad- I was even worried that he was going to kick me out. I was sure that bitch that was his girlfriend would have something to say about it.

Rita was slightly younger than my dad- she was thirty-five. Rita had her own daughter called Angel who was horrible, and she was my youngest brother's mum. She had short brown hair in a bob, and I will give it to her - she was gorgeous, but she was a nasty woman. She just used to snipe at me and was never very nice to me. I begged my dad not to propose to her when he was going to last Christmas. I know that's selfish, but I don't think I could handle her as my step mum.

I pushed the key through the door, and walked in. My dad came rushing towards me.

"Where have you been?" He asked angrily.

"Nowhere." I tried to brush past him.

Rita walked towards me.

"Why are you so rude to your father?"

"Why don't you fuck off." I replied.

"Go upstairs! I'll talk to you when you've stopped being a brat." My dad shouted at me angrily.

I stormed up the stairs and smashed my door open. I hid under the covers of my bed. Tears fell like a waterfall on either side of my face. My life felt like it was over. I was on my own, sixteen, broke, and definitely couldn't return to school. Only Bianca must have known that I was pregnant, and I wanted it to stay that way- I was not going to be telling any of my other friends. I still needed to find a way to tell my dad, and the father of the child. But I was thinking about myself first of all.

A child would give me a purpose in life, it would be the reason I could wake up. I might have been sixteen, but in some ways I was ready. I was ready. I psyched myself up and confidently walked downstairs, and was met in the kitchen by glares from my dad and Rita. I rolled my eyes at Rita and just said it how it was.

"I'm pregnant."

"What?" My dad's jaw dropped. "Tell me you're joking."

"I did a test at Bianca's this morning, and it came back positive."

"You're such an idiot Nicola. Your dad does so much for you, and you repay him by getting up the duff- and now we'll have to pay for this child."

"Rita, respectfully shut your mouth." My dad chimed in.

Yes, I thought. Finally, my dad was standing up to that bitch. She was a nasty woman, and she deserved to be put in her place like that. I was so happy.

"Danny? Don't be so rude."

"You deserve it- you treat my daughter like shit and give your opinions when they're not necessary." He looked sternly at her. "This is between me and *my* daughter. She's not yours. So can you please leave the room."

"God you are just the worst man I have ever come across."

As much as I hated her, I didn't want a domestic to happen while I was telling my dad about me being pregnant. This was not going well.

Rita got up and walked towards the island. There was a small glass cider bottle that my dad must have had earlier in the day. I looked towards the ground, so I didn't make eye contact with her. In a split second, I saw the empty bottle fly over my head towards my dad who ducked. Thankfully it completely missed him, but it hit the wall and smashed everywhere.

"You're crazy." My dad yelled at her.

"No- you are!" She picked up her keys and stormed out of the room. I heard a slam of the front door. I presumed this was another one of her storm outs she had if something wasn't going her way. I'm surprised my dad didn't leave her after that incident- he kicked her out of the house in early 1998, but they were finally over just before Christmas of that year.

"Sorry that you had to see that." He came over to give me a big hug, before telling me to sit down.

"You're going to have to terminate it, Nic. I'm so sorry, but there's no way we can afford to keep this baby. I don't have any money, and I can't take time off work to look after them because you've gone out partying or gone to college."

"I can look after the baby; I promise you dad. I think I'm ready."

"You're 16- you don't need this in your life at the moment. You have your whole life ahead of you. Please don't do this." He looked at me, upset.
"Just think about it. It wouldn't be worth it."

I gave him a hug and walked away. I wiped a tear from my cheek and went up the stairs. The front door was wide open - a usual dramatic Rita move. I was over her behaviour completely- a nasty example of a woman. I slammed the door shut.

Laying there, I thought about all the different options - should I keep this baby? Or not. I had no idea. My brain was in a thousand different places- all I wanted was a solid answer of what to do. My dad was right- this was the start of my life. I didn't want to be tied down to a child for the next sixteen years of my life, or more. I wanted to have a life, I wanted to pursue a career, I wanted to go to college. But then this baby; the guilt would never leave me if I had a termination. I had only known I was pregnant for less than a day, but all these feelings were circling around my head.

The other issue was: I had no idea who the father was. I had no idea.
There were 3 people. Ricky, my on and off boyfriend - he was tall, dark and a fitness freak. He was slightly older than me though (the year above at school). He played rugby and was quite a rough person, but not with me. We

split up in May because he got into a street fight with one of his ex-friends and ended up getting arrested for GBH. The trial was set for that October. I didn't really know what he was up to at the moment- last I heard he was on remand, but I saw him on Hove high street about two weeks ago.

Another potential was Aaron. Aaron was my childhood best friend- my dad and his dad were best friends. He was definitely my favourite choice for a father. He was the same age as me, but had a sense of maturity that the other boys didn't have. Aaron was smart, he was going to do A-levels and was probably going to go to university. He was very tall, but much skinnier than Ricky. He had good features - especially his green eyes. Secretly, I was praying it was him.

The other potential was Harvey. Harvey was a lot older than me - closing in on twenty. He was much scarier than the other two- he was a drug dealer. He ran a cannabis farm in the back of his brother's flat. I wasn't supposed to spill that though. Harvey was much smaller than the other two boys, but he was definitely the one I was most terrified of. Harvey and I had had a short fling in June, only at a few parties we'd been together. I call that my off the rail's era.

I thought for a moment about who the father of this baby could be. A realisation came over me that it didn't really matter who it was- the fact that I didn't know was probably a good reason to get rid of it. It would be likely that I would have to raise the baby on my own, and I definitely couldn't do that. I worked one day a week for four pounds an hour- there was no way I was going to fund this baby. I was definitely realising why my dad didn't want me to keep it- he would have had to pay for it and help me look after it too.

A bang on the door, "Come in."
It was my dad. He came to sit on the edge of my bed.
"Nicola, you are so strong. But this baby would be a total mistake."
"I know dad, but I don't want to live with the guilt for the rest of my life." I replied. I felt a weird mix of emotions.
"I get that- but you have your whole life ahead of you. You have dreams. You have potential. In a few years maybe, when you're able to be financially stable or are in a stable relationship, then it will be your time."
"You're right. I would have been certain to keep it if I knew who the father was." I replied, accidentally saying my thoughts out loud.
"You don't know who the baby's dad is? Nicola!"
"Oops." I knew this would piss him off.
"Right, who knows about this pregnancy?"
"Only Bianca." I looked at my dad, terrified.
"Make sure it stays that way."
In truth I never did check if Bianca had said anything- because I completely blocked her out. I have many regrets

in life- but that is definitely the biggest. I miss her a lot. Like a lot. She did so much for me, but I was scared of facing her.

11

"Come on Nikki, we're going."

"Ok let me get my shoes on, I'll be down in a second."

"Quick, your appointment is in ten minutes."

Today was the day I was getting rid of this baby. It had only been two days that I had known about it though. I didn't even know if the baby was a boy or a girl- I didn't know how far along I was either. I assumed I was about six to eight weeks. I hoped I wasn't much further than that, because there was a lot of guilt hanging over me. I was upset that this whole ordeal had happened. My emotions were heightened completely. I struggled to sleep- at this point a termination would be the best option to end this whole thing.

I tied my laces, and legged it out of the door and into my dad's car.

I was shaking, my legs were numb. My hands were ice blue- the circulation felt like it had been cut off. Despite this, my face was really sweaty.

"You alright?" My dad asked, having one eye on the road and the other on the steering wheel.

"I- I can't stop shaking. I don't know what's come over me."

"Breathe, Nic. Breathe. It will all be over today."

I took a deep breath. "You're right."

He drove up to the clinic- it was hidden behind an industrial estate. He pulled up right outside of it and parked. He got out of the car and mouthed to me "Get out." Through the windscreen.

"I can't." I mouthed back, shaking my head in panic.

He rushed over to my door and pulled it open.

"You've got to do this- you might be nervous, but it's for the best."

I couldn't move- I was paralysed. Something was telling me not to go through with it. I just couldn't move myself- I wanted to get out, but I couldn't.

"I can't move, my body won't let me." I yelled.

"Just breathe Nicola please." I was in floods of tears- a total wreck. My head was pounding, my heart was throbbing. My legs couldn't move. They were just stuck. No movement.

My dad eventually pulled me out of the car, holding on tight to me as we entered the clinic.

"Hi, what's your name?"

"Nicola Mckenna."

"And date of birth?"

"25th March 1981."

The receptionist gasped.

"What's up?" My dad asked.

"You're just so young. I thought you would be older."

"Well, you must get younger here."

"No, we do, but you look older than sixteen- I was certain you were going to be born in the 70s."

"Isn't that a bit unprofessional?"

The receptionist looked at my dad blankly.

"Your appointment is in Room 2 on the left."

"Thank you." My dad answered for me.

My dad walked in first, and I followed him in. The room was a blank white room with a hospital-like bed and a woman sat by the desk. She was wearing scrub and had bright blonde hair that was tied up in a ponytail. She must have been in her early thirties, maybe slightly younger.

"Hey, you must be Nicola. Please, sit down."

"Hi." I said shakily.

"Oh, you mustn't be nervous." She tried to reassure me.

"We will talk through whether this is the best option, or if there is another option that would best suit your needs. Is this your dad?"

"Yes, he's my dad." My dad tightly held my hand.

"Ok great. I'm glad you've got someone supportive to be here." She smiled at me with big, white, shiny teeth. Definitely veneers.

"So, what we're going to do is talk through it- I'm going to speak to you on your own as well, and then we'll decide from there."

"Thank you." I replied.

"First of all. Why are you here?"

"I found out I was pregnant two days ago, and I'm only sixteen years old. I don't really want to keep this baby at all." I was lying through my teeth. I wanted this baby, but

94

it just wasn't logical to keep it, and I wasn't financially stable. "And I don't know who the dad is."

"Ok. Well, it isn't uncommon for this to happen to girls your age. Did you use protection?"

"Yes, this is why it's so confusing."

"Don't worry- it happens. It's not your fault."

When she said that, all I felt like doing was sobbing right in front of her. But I needed to stay strong for myself, and for my dad.

"So, we have three options, you can get a termination today. Or you can decide against having one. Or we can book you in for a checkup to be within the next three weeks."

"Ok." I was trying to process everything as she spoke to me. It was a whole lot of information to take in.

"Now we need to have a chat on your own without your dad."

"That's ok, can you wait outside for me dad?"

"Course, see you in a minute."

As the door shut, the woman's look became more serious. "What do you really want to do? Be honest with me please."

"In some ways I want to keep the baby, but I also don't at the same time. I'm just totally confused. I'm scared that I will live with so much guilt from getting rid of it. But at the same time, I don't want to, because I know it would prevent me from having a successful life."

"You know, whatever you do will be the right decision for you and your path."

"I just want to please my dad- I don't want him to have the stress of this baby. He would have to provide for it, since I don't know who the baby's father is."

"Is there any way you could tell who the father could be?"

"No. This summer has been such a blur."

"Nicola, do you think you know what option you're going to choose?"

"I'm going to abort the baby."

12

'Sorry, dad.'

'I can't believe this. How have you managed to get pregnant again? I thought you would have learnt from two and a half years ago.'

'I'm sorry. But I'm keeping it this time.'

The flashbacks of the summer of 1997 were in the forefront of my mind. I was not going to live with the guilt of a second abortion- I just couldn't lose another child.

'What??'

'Yeah- I'm eighteen weeks along already.'

'Oh Nikki, I can't believe this. I don't know whether to be really mad or really happy. You only left for London last week- you're going to have to come back.'

'I'm not going to leave dad- I'm going to try and find a flat and live on my own.'

'How? And with what money?'

'I just will- I'll make it work dad I promise'

'And while I've got you, why did I see you in the Sunday newspaper with your tongue down some random footballers throat?'

'It's a long story, dad - I'm too stressed to get into it right now.'

'We can talk again tomorrow when you've calmed down.'

'Thanks dad.'

'Bye Nic.'

'Bye dad.'

The phone call ends. I threw my phone into my bag and crashed into bed. I was asleep for about an hour and a half, before I was woken up by yet another bang on the door. Thinking it was Rochelle, I called out "Come in."

Romeo walked in. I looked at him in disgust.

"What do you want? I don't want to speak to you."
"Can I not even have a chance to explain?" He looked remorseful.
"Why did you do it? I have never been exposed to the press before. I wouldn't be surprised if I get hounded when I leave the house just because you wanted to make some dosh."
"I didn't do it for the money."
"Why then?"
"I did it to distract the papers from something else. I wasn't going to do it, until I got a tip off from one of the journalists that they were going to run a story on me."
"What was the story?" I was over his excuses by this point- too many lies and too much deceit.
"I don't really know how to say it."
"Spit it out. Or get out."
"They- they were going to run a story about me kissing a man."
I was stunned. I wasn't expecting that. Romeo was gay? Big macho Romeo. I could not believe what I was hearing. This was just too much to take all in one go. Never in a

million years would I have guessed that. I didn't know whether to be angry or upset with him.

"So you're gay then?"

"Yeah, basically."

"Oh my god."

Why did he take me on a date? Why did he kiss me? Why did I end up in his bed?

"Are you even attracted to me?"

"Yes, that's why I kissed you twice."

"Oh. Right." It was time for me to be honest. I needed to get it out there, it was bugging me.

"Why did I wake up in your bed then?"

"Oh yeah, that's because you crashed in bed. That's probably why you can't remember it. Nothing happened. I'm only into guys."

I was reeling. I couldn't handle all this information at once. I didn't hate Romeo anymore, I understood why he had done it. I was still mad about being on the front page of everywhere- but that story could have destroyed his career.

"I'm so sorry Nikki, I feel like a fraud. My behaviour's been bang out of order. I want to make it up to you. I want to help you look after this baby; I'll pay for it all - you won't have to pay for any of it.

I just need a favour from you: that you pretend to be my girlfriend."

"What! Are you joking? I definitely don't think that's a good idea."

Was he actually suggesting that we fake a relationship so he doesn't get outed?

"It would help you with your dream to be a glamour model, and you can come live with me in my house in Newcastle."

"Why should I? I've just started this new life in London, and you want me to move up to Newcastle with you. You've already exposed me to the papers. Now I have to continue this media presence."

"I know it sounds awful- but it would help both of us." I was genuinely shell shocked. Completely stunned. My life would change yet again, and I'd have to move up north. Another new start. I hadn't even spoken to Rochelle or Andre about this- I didn't want to out Romeo in case either of them didn't know. But at the same time, I needed advice from Rochelle. I needed to talk to somebody about all these bombshells - it was constant, literally one after the other. I just couldn't take it anymore.

"Does your brother know?" I asked.

"No. But Rochelle does."

"How?"

"She caught me a few weeks back, someone had come round the house."

"Wow. How did she react?"

"She was more shocked than you are. She couldn't believe it, but she promised she would keep it a secret from Andre. I needed to make sure none of my immediate family found out."

"Your brother runs a salon, I'm sure he would be accepting." I laughed. Probably wasn't a funny joke to make though.

"You're right, but I'd be more worried about my parents finding out, and then everyone else - my uncles, aunties, grandparents and all the rest of them."

"Why? we're in 2000 now."

"Because they wouldn't be accepting -a gay footballer? Never."

"And what about you? Rochelle said to me in the car that you're out."

"Yeah, she's not happy I dragged you into all this. She's actually really angry because she wanted to make sure no one else got caught up in my lies."

"Are you going to leave then?"

"Yes. Tomorrow morning, I'll be back next week though- but the choice is yours. You can come with me next week up to Newcastle, and I'll pay for the baby. I'll pay for your whole life. We can get a nanny in; I just need you to pretend to be my girlfriend."

I sat there, staring into space. Then I started wondering about whether or not his exes knew.

"Does your ex-wife know? And what about Pandora?"

"How do you know about Pandora?"

"Rochelle told me."

"Ugh- well I had to pay Pandora off because she tried to expose my secret."

"How much did you pay her?" I was intrigued.

"Best part of 150k."

My jaw dropped.

"What the hell?"

"I know. We had a short fling, but then she found out about it so she tried to expose me." He had his head in his hands. "It turned messy quickly: I sold pictures of us to the tabloids, she threatened to sell my story. She has a journalist on speed dial."

"On speed dial?"

"Yes. She sent me letters saying that if I mentioned her in the press or said anything about her, in any way, she would sell the story immediately."

"She sounds toxic. But I want to meet her."

"You want to meet her?"

"Yes - I want to know her side of the story."

"Why?"

"Because I want to know how she handled fame-especially if I'm going to have to live with it."

I knew being interested in meeting her was going to cause an issue, but I was still really mad about being plastered on the front page of every national newspaper, just because Romeo wanted to cover up his own secrets. I was being used as a pawn.

I knew I could use this to my advantage though, because this could be my big break. Obviously, I couldn't be a glamour model if I was pregnant, but I still could still get my name out there in the media. That definitely makes me sound like I was using Romeo- but I needed him just as much as he needed me.

"I'll definitely consider it Romeo. I need money for this baby- I can't raise it on my own. I know this isn't your child, but you can help me."

"I will. I need you, Nicola. And I know you're young, but you have something that could be really good for modelling."

"I just don't want to be the one who has to pick up the pieces that you leave behind when I go up there.
I think it could work though."

Something was telling me to go with him. I had only moved to London just over a week ago, but this was like a second new start, and too many dramas had happened in the last two weeks. I did wonder if I would be a long way away from home. I had never been to Newcastle and to be honest, I didn't know where it was. I was hoping it wasn't too far away from London- or especially Brighton.

"Where is Newcastle?"
"About four hours away from here."
"What!"
"Where did you think it was?"
"I don't know- I just didn't think it was that far away."
"It's quite different from here. I like it though. There is a smaller gay scene up there so there's not much to do."
"I'll think about it, Romeo. I promise."

Romeo walked out of the room, And I was stunned by the
news he had just given me. Romeo was a nice boy- I had a
lot more respect for him now. He offered to provide for
my child. It was almost a no brainer.

But there were a lot of hurdles to get through to that point.
I needed to speak to Rochelle for advice- I don't think
she'd be very happy if I told her I was going to live with
Romeo after what he did to me. But I knew the struggle
that Romeo was going through- I had a friend who was
gay, and I remembered how he was an outcast at school,
but then I saw how happy he was in the middle of
Brighton around other gay people. Romeo's situation
reminded me about that friend and his struggles.

That friend taught me a lot about being resilient. His name
was Jordan. Jordan was there for me through every point
of my life, but I sometimes couldn't be there for him when
he was getting beaten up. He came out the other side of
secondary school a much stronger person- I knew the
struggle Romeo must be going through right now.

The news was just unexpected from Romeo, A six foot
five, footballer, muscly. It was just a shock. He wasn't
very feminine either, although I shouldn't stereotype. He
was very good at hiding it as well- all these ex-girlfriends.
He must have been really struggling with it all.

In other ways though, I was upset. I was being used as a
pawn in a game with the press. I think it was all a bit too
much all at once- how could an eighteen-year-old girl

handle all this? Obviously, there were people who were suffering more than me in the world, but I had managed to land myself in a right mess.

I walked into the kitchen downstairs to find Rochelle sitting alone with the daily newspaper and a cup of coffee. She was probably reading about me- I was hoping she wasn't but I genuinely didn't know what to expect at this point.

"Hey Nikki. Are you alright?"

"Yeah you? What are you reading about?"

"Oh, just the latest news about Iraq."

"Iraq? What's happening in Iraq?"

"They say there might be a war or something like that."

"Oh right. Wow."

"So, did Romeo speak to you then?" She really got to the point quickly.

"He explained everything. In some ways, I understand why he did it."

"I don't." She scoffed. "I think what he did was so wrong- and what he did to Pandora."

"Yeah, I guess. But surely you have to sympathise with him a bit- imagine what mental turmoil that he's going through. He can't accept himself. I have friends who are gay, and it's soul destroying to see what they have to go through on a daily basis."

"I don't get it. He's selfish. You shouldn't be brushing this off so easily. You were on the front page- why are you being so complacent?"

"He offered to pay for everything for me and the baby."
"He did what?"
I wasn't going to repeat myself to her- I knew she had heard me. I could tell she was getting quite irate about it, not sure why though.
"Yeah, he's going to pay for everything and move me up to Newcastle with him."
"Why does he need you in Newcastle- can't he just send the cheques to you down south?"
"Well, there's something I have to do for him."
"What is it?"
"I have to fake a relationship with him for the British newspapers."
"What the fuck. He's crazy, I swear. Stay well away from him. You'd fuck up everything that's going for you."

She gave me the dirtiest look I've ever received in my life. This was a completely different side to Rochelle that I had never ever seen before- it was like she was two different people; the nice one I knew when we went on that day out to London together, and whoever was talking to me now. Why did she try to set me up with Romeo then? Why did everyone have an ulterior motive? People were ruthless and too many people were showing their true colours.
"I think it would work for me- he said he'd help me make it as a glamour model."
"Oh my god. He's lying. You won't be a glamour model. You're gorgeous Nicola, but he won't help you. He will drop you when this media firestorm is over and he's

avoided it, whenever you're no longer of use to him. He will send you back off to London without a penny. Watch it. Don't do it. Actually, you can do what you want- but you won't be welcome back here if you go. Sorry."

"Romeo is literally your brother-in-law- why do you hate him so much?"

"Pandora worked in my salon."

"Really? I had no idea."

"Yeah, and then Romeo got involved and basically destroyed her life- like he did to you and will continue to do."

"I think my life was already destroyed by my own actions - I'm eighteen weeks pregnant."

"True- but it just resonates with me because she suffered the same thing. She was one of my best hair stylists, and a good friend of mine. He decided it was a good idea to enter a relationship with her, and then the pictures in the press came out- I was livid. He lied to me about why he had done it, until I came home to find him and another man sitting in the kitchen. I was absolutely enraged."

"I didn't know Pandora worked for you."

"Yeah, and I had to lose her- she couldn't keep working at my salon if she was on the front page of the papers. And now it's happened again with you."

She had a sense of evil in her eyes- she was definitely staring into my soul. It was a complete contrast to the person I thought I had known her to be. I was just confused by all of this- I think I was in way too deep and couldn't seem to get myself out of this mess. The man I liked was gay, and he wanted me to falsely be in a relationship with him. My cousin, who I was living with, and thought was lovely, was actually quite aggressive. And to top it all off, I was pregnant with a baby, and I had no idea who the father was.

All I knew was that I needed to get back home, fast.

13

I started to pack my bags even though it was the middle of the night. I pulled out my suitcase from under my bed and threw all the clothes from my wardrobe into it, not really caring how I folded it or how organised it was. I just knew I needed to get out of here.

The clock by the side of my bed said 1am. I had to escape without anyone knowing. Well except Romeo- I needed him to act as a decoy to get me out. I was going to go back to Brighton- I needed to get my head back in the right place. I was a mess: I needed to make up my mind about whether I was going to go with Romeo- I needed money and he was offering it. Obviously, I didn't want to anger Rochelle by leaving, but it was the right thing for me, and I didn't think she'd understand. As I was packing, I heard a knock on the door. I shoved the suitcase under the bed again - half packed and with clothes flying out of the sides of it. I was really hoping it wasn't Rochelle or Andre, because it would mean my plan would have been foiled and I would have gotten into so much trouble.

"It's only me Nicola, don't worry." It was Romeo- I was so relieved. "How are we planning on getting you out of here?"

"I don't know- but I need you to distract them by blocking the stairs, while I'll try and sneak out of the front door." The plan sounded completely lame, I knew that, but I was just desperate to get out of this house as soon as possible. I wasn't going to wait around any longer.

"I just need to get out of here. I need to go back home and sort out my head." I said to Romeo, with tears in my eyes.
"This is all my fault." He replied, looking visibly upset.
"It's not, Romeo- I understand what you're going through."
"I know I'm just inflicting my problem onto everyone else- it's not fair to you Nickki."
"Yeah, but I couldn't even imagine the stress of what you're going through.
I have to go back home so I can decide whether or not I'll follow you to Newcastle."
"I understand."
"Thank you."
He shuts the door behind him, and I continue to pack all my clothes into the suitcase. The suitcase was full, and I hadn't even packed everything. It was probably best to leave a couple of outfits, as a parting gift. I struggled to zip up my suitcase quietly, but managed to shove all of my clothes down. I carried it out of the door and put it outside of the door, slowly closing it behind me. This was definitely going to be the last time I was going to be in that room- something told me I was not going to be welcome back here anytime soon. I tiptoed quietly down the stairs, trying to not make a creak. Romeo followed me just a second later and opened the front door for me.
"Bye Nic- good luck."
"See you soon, Romeo."
The door shut. I turned to face it one last time, and walked away

14

I walked towards the train station. It was dark - I could barely see. Only streetlights were guiding me towards where I needed to go. The streets were dead, only a few cats out patrolling the pavements and a couple of motorbikes zooming down - probably drug fixers. I was alone, lost and pregnant. It wasn't where I was expecting to be at my age, especially ten days after I moved to London. My suitcase bumped over every crack in the pavement. How was my life such a mess? That question constantly played over my head. How did this all happen? I needed to plan what I was going to do next, I needed advice from my family, I needed advice from my friends. I wanted to see what they thought about me going with Romeo- I knew I could trust my dad and my two closest friends, but I obviously didn't want to out Romeo to anyone- that wasn't me.

I ran up to the departure boards, but there was only one left, and it was to London Victoria. I got on the train as it pulled into the platform. It was like the end of a chapter in my life - a very hectic ten days that I was still reeling from. The train carriage was exactly the same as the one that I had been on when I arrived, and when I went into London with Rochelle. It was drab with dried chewing gum everywhere. The difference was this time I was in an empty carriage- I mean who would be getting on a train on a Monday night at one in the morning. I felt my eyes close as I was sitting on the seat. I wanted to forget all that had happened to me over the last few days- I was so tired. I was exhausted in fact.

*

I walked off the train at Victoria. It was deserted. I have never ever seen a place so big, so empty. I could only see a cleaner who was sweeping up. My train was the only one that was in the station at this point, which filled me with worry. The barriers were wide open, so I walked straight through. I looked up at the departure board - it was blank. No Gatwick express, no trains to Brighton. No trains going anywhere out of London. It was hopeless- I was either going to have to find a hotel, or sleep on a bench in the station. I didn't have the money for a hotel though- I only had a ten-pound note left in my bag. It was dire.

A bench for a bed? I was pregnant. This was not a good place for me to sleep- I would be awake all night. Why couldn't I have escaped earlier? I would have got back to Hove if I had left just an hour before. It was going to be a long night. I found a bench in the corner by the same Boots I bought the meal deal from when I first arrived. I sat down and waited- I decided it was best not to fall asleep as I didn't know what was going to happen. I had my suitcase close by- I needed to make sure it wasn't stolen. The cleaner who was sweeping the floor walked towards me.

"Hiya, what are you waiting for?"

"I missed the last train to Brighton- do you know when the next train is going to be?"

"Yes, it's 4:50am. Are you going to wait there?"

"Yeah, I have to- I have no money to get a hotel."

"What's your story- why are you here?"

"To be honest, I don't really know where to start."

The cleaner gave me a look.

"Were you on the front of the newspaper?"

Oh god, how did she recognise me? I have gone through hell and back, the last thing I needed was some cleaner recognising me. For all I know, she could go to the press and sell a story on me if I told her anything.

"Love, you were, weren't you?"

"Yes. I was."

"Are you famous?"

"Definitely not. I didn't even want to be on the front page, I'm literally eighteen years old."

"What? Really?"

"Yes."

"I can't believe that- you're so young! How did you end up on the front page?"

"I went on a date with a footballer."

"Ah… yes I saw that footballer, he was here a few weeks ago actually."

"Really?"

"Yeah, I spoke to him - he was very nice."

Why was this cleaner telling me all of this? I was finding this a really awkward conversation.

"What did you speak to him about?"

"Nothing much- he was right here on this bench when I was sweeping."

I genuinely thought this woman was crazy, why was she telling me this? I wanted to be nice- but I was really too tired to care. That makes me sound like an awful, awful person - but can you blame me? My life is a whirlwind. I'm knackered.

"Oh, that's really lovely."

"Yes. I'll stop bothering you now." She must have got the hint. I felt guilty though- I probably sounded quite fake.

"No, don't go. Sit down." I ushered her back. "What's your name?" I was just trying to be polite.

"My name is Denise." She smiled at me.

"Denise, how are you?"

"I'm alright. I mean, my life isn't going anywhere. I'm fifty-seven and I clean a train station on my own."

"Why do you do this job? I'm not trying to be rude, but I feel like you could do better."

"There are no jobs around here anymore. I've worked here for about three years, but there are so many people in London now that there are no jobs."

"I didn't know."

"It's been a really tough time- I'm considering moving out of London."

I did feel bad for Denise, she sounded a bit depressed. I wanted to help her as much as I could, but my energy levels were just too low to try. I was so sleep deprived- it was past 2am.

I comforted Denise as best as I could.

"It'll be alright."

A voiceover in the station announced it was 2:30am.

"Oh, I've got to go. Thank you for talking to me." She said.

"My pleasure." I smiled at her. She walked away, and I lay back in the seat. I felt my eyes close, and I drifted off to sleep.

*

I jolted awake. I could see people walking past me, and I looked up towards the time and it said 6:05am. I gasped. I felt like I couldn't breathe. How did I fall asleep? What happened? I still had my suitcase right next to me - I was certain it would have been stolen. How could I have been so careless to have fallen asleep? With a suitcase as well. I needed a minute to work out what I was going to do next. I mean I had literally been sleeping on a bench- my eyelashes were still stuck to each other, and I could barely see anything. My vision was blurred. I stood up, grabbed my suitcase, and ran towards the board. It said there was a train in just under eight minutes to Brighton. I rushed around to find a ticket machine. I used my last ten-pound note. I was going to have to jump the train between Haywards Heath and Brighton- I didn't have enough money to pay all the way. This was going to be chaotic, but I needed to get home as soon as possible.

I rushed onto the platform and ran onto the train. It was quite a busy train (not sure why, it was half six in the morning). I found a small seat, right at the end of the carriage. It was quite cramped with my suitcase and my bag. I was glad to be leaving- I had loved my first week in London, but it was all ruined by all the drama of the last 72 hours. I wanted to see my dad, I wanted to see my friends and I wanted to see my brothers and sister. These ten days had been a wild experience. I was also going to have to work out who the father of the baby was. It was something I had blocked out of my brain - originally, I thought it must have been Ricky - it seemed to be the only viable option. But finding out how far along I was made me think it could have been someone else. It could either be Aaron (who I had also been off and on with, but he had always been one of my best friends) or it could be Joel. Joel worked at the leisure centre with me- he was one of the personal trainers. He was drop dead gorgeous - I mean even more than Romeo, but we had had only a short fling. He was muscular, tall, really tanned (borderline orange though).

Any of these three could have been the dad- to be honest I didn't know how I could let history repeat itself with another pregnancy, another pregnancy where I had no idea who the father was. This exact same scenario mirrored that of my short-lived pregnancy when I was sixteen. I regretted having the termination, but I also knew it had been the best for me at the time. That baby could have potentially had a drug dealer for a dad. It would have hurt my life prospects- I was selfish, but I felt pressure from my own dad at that point in my life to do it. I didn't want the same thing to happen again - I wasn't going to let him dictate my life now. I was an adult, I needed to make my own decisions. I stared out of the window as we left London, realising this was the end of my time here for who knows how long.

*

We pulled out of Haywards Heath station, and the ticket checker came walking along. I locked eyes with him. My hands started shaking rapidly- I knew this was going to happen. Just my luck. Had I not faced enough in the last few days. This must be some kind of karma, why was I constantly being punished? The ticket checker continued to get closer, as people continued to flash their tickets. By this point, I had accepted my fate. I was going to get dumped off this train at the next station- I didn't even know where I was. I was ready to run, ready to go. But I didn't- I stayed right there.

He strode right up to me.
"Tickets please."
I froze. I couldn't speak, I couldn't move.

"Er… Um. Well."

"You don't have it do you?"

"N-no."

"Right, you do know it's illegal to not pay the train fare."

"Yes. But I didn't have any money, and I needed to get home."

"That doesn't make it any less illegal, who do you think you are?" He looked irate.

"I'm sorry."

I was mortified- the whole train carriage was staring directly at me, watching my every move. I could hear whispers about me not paying for the train fare. "Chav." I heard one old woman mutter.

The train guard looked at me in disappointment. "I'll let you stay on the train, but I'm going to have to impose a fixed penalty notice on you."

I had no idea what that was. I didn't really want to know though; it didn't sound good.

"What is that?"

"You don't know… it's a fine, it's eighty pounds."

Was he having a laugh? How was I going to find that kind of money anywhere?

"Right… ok." I stuttered.

"I need you to give me your address so the head office can send you the fine."

"I don't know my address."

"If you don't give me an address, you could be prosecuted."

He was quite a scary person, so I gave him my address without a single thought. After that, he walked straight off without another word.

I got off the train at Brighton- the ordeal was over. I was home. I hadn't told anyone that I was back though, I hadn't even checked my phone - it was dead. I ran through the train station and through the barriers. Thank God the barriers were open, I don't think I could have handled another stop by another railway worker. I rushed out of the station. The time was 8am- I was ready to get home. It was a Tuesday morning, the commuters were rushing around, trying to barge past me as I exited the station and down the stairs.

I turned onto the street, and I started lugging my suitcase along. The walk dragged on and on. The sky was grey, bleak and depressing. This was my life now. Trickles of rain hit my hair- I was a mess. I only had four hours of sleep, and even then, I was sleeping on a bench. I also knew I looked like I had had four hours sleep. I had just been fined on the train home- everything for me was going wrong, I needed to get it back on track as soon as possible.

*

I walked up the hill towards my house. I took one look at it and thought, how the hell am I back here so early? I knocked on the door.

My dad opened it- he looked straight at me and said nothing.

"Hi dad."

He ran up and gave me a hug.

"I'm so glad you're home, Nikki."

"So am I Dad. I've missed you."

"Come in, we need to talk." He ushered me straight into the living room- he didn't even give me a chance to put my stuff upstairs or have a wash.

I sat down on the sofa in the living room, and to be honest I was surprised I didn't immediately fall asleep on it.

"So, you told me you're pregnant again?"

"Dad, do we have to do this now? I've had an awful night trying to get back here- I just want to collapse in my bed and go to sleep."

"Ok I understand- we'll talk later."

"Thanks, dad"

He swiftly exited the room while I dragged my suitcase up the stairs back into my old bedroom. I gasped a sigh of relief- I was so glad to be back.

My room was just as I left it, my pillows were arranged in the way I liked them, my bed was made, and nothing had been touched. I was glad to be able to sleep in my own bed- nothing will ever beat the feeling of your own bed after being away. I fell on top of my duvet, and my eyes slammed shut.

15

The sun peeked through my window, and I jolted awake. My first reaction was to look at the clock- it was 3:30 pm. My brain was blank for a second, until it started filling up with all of the dramas of the last few days. My hands started shaking again, along with my legs. I felt a cold spark shiver down my spine. My dad had wanted to speak to me about the pregnancy, and why I was back. How was I supposed to explain to him everything that had happened with Romeo, and that I didn't know who the father of my child was. Oh, and let's not forget the incident where I got fined on the train this morning? It was a whirlwind, but at the same time it felt so long ago. I thought it would be good to take my mind off of things by calling one of my friends.

I picked up my phone, which I must have put on charge before I went to sleep (although I don't remember doing so). I had four new messages- my heart sank. I had a gut feeling one of them at least was going to be from Rochelle. It turned out all four of them were from her:
'*Why have you left? I literally let you into my home, and let you stay. And you just bolted.*'
'*I don't think you understand how mad I actually am.*'
'*I am livid, Nicola.*'
'*Reply to me bitch.*'
All of them were definitely quite nasty, and I immediately pressed the bin button on my phone- I even went as far as

binning her contact as well. That was quite a harsh move, as she had done a lot for me in London, but I still didn't deserve verbal abuse from her. My brain went into overdrive- I felt a wave of guilt and anxiety over seeing that message. She was my cousin after all; I wasn't expecting her to react like this. I then put my phone away, I was too upset to ring Alexandra, or Bonnie for that matter. I just wanted to lie there and cry and cry. How did my life turn out like this? I had managed to alienate basically everyone I knew- well, everyone except Romeo. Even then, I was slightly heartbroken about the fact that mine and Romeo's relationship was all false. It was all getting too much to handle at this point. There was only so much I could take- I felt tears start streaming down my cheeks. I was breathing quite rapidly, and I felt myself gasping for air. Something felt like it was blocking the flow of air in the back of my throat. I couldn't swallow. I was frozen- I didn't want to move. Each of my worries were spinning around my head, occupying every last bit of my brain. It was like I was in a constant state of panic. What was going to happen next in my life? It was all so unpredictable.

A bang on the door; my dad burst in.
"Nicola, what's wrong? Why are you breathing so heavily?"
"I-I don't k-know but it won't stop." The words struggled to get out of me.
"What's happening? This isn't normal- this isn't like you."

I just stared back at him blankly - I could barely move.

"Do we need to get you to the hospital?"

"N-no. I've just got back. I'm sure I'll be alright."

"You look really pale; we're going to need to take you to the hospital now. You need to get help as soon as possible."

"What about the kids?"

"I'll call Pixie from next door; she can look after them." Pixie was just a bit younger than me- she was a lovely girl, who couldn't do enough for the people around her. I always worried about her because her friends were quite fake and she was very timid and shy, but she would always look after my younger siblings if me or my dad were ever out.

*

Dad drove us into the hospital car park, and I still couldn't breathe properly. My whole body was shaking - but I still think dad was overreacting about going to the hospital. I didn't think I was ill- probably just stressed or tired.

"Get out of the car." He shouted.

"Ok, ok." I replied.

I slammed the car door shut and walked towards the hospital entrance. The sliding doors opened up and my dad brought me along to the reception. I must have looked quite pale, because the hospital receptionist didn't even ask me to wait- she organised a doctor to see me straight away.

"Room six please." She pointed straight at the door behind her. I walked along, a couple of steps behind my dad. He knocked on the door.

"Come in." A man in scrubs opened it; he was quite tall, three or four inches taller than my dad, and must have been a similar age. "Take a seat, both of you."

I sat down, although I almost missed the seat - that would have just added to the embarrassment.

"So, what can I help you with?" He asked.

"My daughter," My dad gestured at me. "She can't stop shaking, and she's breathing heavily."

"And how long has this been going on for?"

"I think maybe thirty minutes." He answered for me.

"Right, it looks like she's having a panic attack."

"What's a panic attack?" My dad asked.

"It's a relatively new term: it's to do with the pathways in her brain. It's only temporary and is usually caused by a stressful event or memory. Is there anything that you think could be causing this?" He turned towards me.

"Er... too-too much."

"Where do you want to start?"

"I-I don't want to go into it." I really didn't want to tell this random doctor about all the things that were going on in my life such as the pregnancy, the dramas with Rochelle, and let's not forget being fined on the train. He didn't really need to know about all this chaos. Nor did my dad- I hadn't said any of it to him yet because I had only got home a few hours ago. It was still too raw to start talking about it. I knew at one point I would have to tell him, but I wanted to sort it all out on my own.

"You don't have to tell us, but we could get you some therapy. Would that be good?"

"What's that?"

"It's where you can speak about your emotions and talk to someone about what's stressing you out- I think it would be good for you." He turned to dad. "Do you think that would be OK?"

"Absolutely." My dad agreed.

"Great. We'll send you a letter with the next steps- we can get you in to see a therapist on Thursday. Is that alright?"

"Perfect, thank you so much."

*

I lay in my room, wondering what therapy was. What was I going to have to do? Was I going to have to be really open about my struggles? I didn't really know what to expect, but I wasn't looking forward to it. I had never heard of it in my life, so it must have been quite a new thing that they were bringing in, but I didn't want to talk about my feelings or thoughts to anyone, I'd rather just keep them to myself and not cause problems because that's just the way I am. I knew dad wanted to know but I wasn't ready to tell him. I wanted to tell my friends and ask for their advice, but I was too scared to do that as well in case they looked at me differently. If I went ahead with it and the secret got out, I would be branded a bad person and a scrounger for using Romeo's money- but then I was doing him a favour. My mind was completely torn: I knew I could have been making the worst decision in my entire life, but I wanted to keep this baby and run away from all the dramas. Newcastle was going to bring more dramas if I went though, I could just feel it.

16

I got out of bed, pushed my duvet cover off me and opened my curtains. It was a very bleak day; dark grey clouds filled the sky, and rain splashed onto the frame of my window. It was just after 7:45 am, and it was Thursday. I had been home for three days now, and the last two days had been much calmer. I was still avoiding the conversation with my dad about all that was going on in my life. I didn't need him to know. Rochelle was still spamming my number. I sent her a message back on Tuesday- that turned out to be a huge mistake because she then started spamming me with horrible messages back. I just told her how it was- that I couldn't be there (but I thanked her and said I was grateful for her allowing me to stay in her house).

Today was the day that I was going to see this therapist person, and I didn't want to go. I didn't want to open up about my feelings or tell them anything about my life. My dad was really happy that I was going to speak to someone, and that I was getting the help that he says I need. I didn't know what to expect though, was it going to be in a hospital? I knew a couple of people who had had therapy for addictions or mental disorders, but I didn't think I had anything wrong with myself mentally. Well, I must do if they have referred me to therapy. My appointment was at 9am, which I personally thought was quite early- I didn't know what it would entail but I didn't want to be there very long. I didn't want them to psychoanalyse me, but I had no experience that would tell me otherwise.

I took a deep breath and walked downstairs. I hadn't put any makeup on or made any effort to look good.

"Nicola, are you ready to go?"

"Yeah dad, I am. Have the kids gone to school?"

"Yes, Rita dropped them off this morning."

"Rita?" Oh god I thought: how is she back in the picture? I didn't want that witch back in my life- she was a nasty piece of work.

"Oh, don't worry, we're not back together. The restraining order was up so she offered to help, and I needed it."

Yes, dad did have to take a restraining order out on that crazy woman because she threw a bottle at him, and when they broke up, she stalked him. It was a stressful time- court cases among other things. I'm not sure why my dad was trusting someone who has done those things to him, but I was just going to try and ignore it for today.

"Right, ok."

"Get in the car, I'll be out in a second." He said to me.

I stepped into my shoes and walked out towards the car. I swung open the door with such power that it almost hit me. I waited in the car for a while, checking myself in the car wing mirror to see if I actually looked a state, or if I was overreacting. A bit of both I think. Dad got into the car and quickly fastened his seatbelt, and we drove off.

The car journey lasted a while- we must have been quite a way out of Brighton by now because the houses and concrete had turned into hills and grass. Where was this place? It seemed like it was in the middle of nowhere.

"Where are we going, dad?"

"Oh, it's only in Horsham."

"Horsham? That's so random."

"It's supposed to be the best in the area."

"Do you have to pay for this?"

"Yes, I do. But it comes from a sum of money I received recently."

I didn't bother to question him on where this suspicious sum of money had come from, because with all the stress of this therapy appointment I had barely registered what he was saying.

We approached Horsham, and it reminded me of Beckenham but different- it was slower paced. Less motorbikes ploughing down the high street, for one. Horsham itself was actually quite pretty- it was a nice little town. Not somewhere I'd personally choose to move to, but nonetheless, I liked it.

Dad turned down a backroad and drove up a dirt path to this big house. It didn't look like a clinic or somewhere that you would go for medical help, it looked like a family home - it was painted white, with big windows and a large garden that circled the house. The door was made of thick wood - I tried to push it open, but it was really heavy, so dad had to push it open for me. It was a bit embarrassing. From the moment I walked in, I wanted to leave immediately. The whole place was decorated in marble and white, and it was all so clean- pretty much spotless. There was a huge chandelier in the middle of the entrance that nearly blinded me. We turned left and entered a reception area, which was equally as clean and as marble as the rest of the place.

"Hi. How can I help?" The woman on the desk looked up from her computer with a shining white smile almost as bright as the walls around her. Everyone in this place was oh-too clean and polished - it was weird, like nothing I had ever seen before.

"We've got an appointment for my daughter- her name is Nicola."

"Yes, I see. Nicola, can you follow me please? I'll show you where to go. And you can wait in the foyer- there's biscuits and a coffee machine in there."

"Ok, thank you." Dad replied.

I followed this woman along yet another bright white corridor. She was wearing black heel boots that were clomping on the floor, making such a horrible noise. The boots must have added a good three or four inches to her height- she was towering over me. She pointed to the door on her left, which had a sign saying Dr. Zoe Bell on the front.

"This is your room, Nicola."

"Thank you, should I knock?" I was confused.

"No, you can just walk in. Dr. Zoe is one of our best- she's so lovely."

"Ok."

I pushed open the door.

"You alright?" A skinny looking woman spun around on her chair to face me; she had blonde hair in a bob and must've been mid 30s.

"Hiya." I tried not to seem nervous.

"Come and have a seat. And we can begin."

I sat down- the seat was really uncomfortable, it felt like I was sitting on a rock. I was overthinking everything at that moment.

"So, how can I help you, Nicola?" She asked. I thought that was quite a broad question and didn't really know how to respond.

"I've just been feeling really stressed out- it's all happened in the last few days really. I think I was alright up until maybe Friday of last week, six days ago."

"What happened on Friday?"

"Do you promise to keep this a secret?" I said to her seriously.

"Yes of course." She replied earnestly. She seemed like she was a trustworthy person, I could just tell. I knew I couldn't be this easily trusting - but she was a professional. It was her job.

"Well, I went out with this footballer from Newcastle. His name is Romeo. I don't know if you've heard of him?"

"I don't follow football."

"He's always in the tabloids."

"I don't read the news."

"Good." I was really happy, because it meant I wasn't really spilling secrets, because Dr. Zoe didn't know who he was. "Well, he's quite a bit older than me, and he took me on a date to Mayfair. He paid for everything, and it was quite a nice date. Although me and him did have a few heated debates at the dinner table- but I mean who doesn't?"

"So true. Carry on."

"So, when we left the restaurant, he told me to kiss him- so I did. What I didn't realise is that there had actually been a camera, and we got papped."

"Ok, and what happened with the picture?"

"It was on the front page of every newspaper. I didn't realise until I walked into a newsagents and saw pictures of me splashed across the entire newsstand."

"Tell me, Nicola. How did that feel?"

I was quite uncomfortable with that question, but also confused as I didn't really know how I felt in the moment when it happened. I think because I collapsed, I couldn't really recall the moments before.

"Well, I don't know." I explained. "I collapsed at the sight of it."

"Why?"

"The doctors said it was due to shock and combined with the fact that I was having bad morning sickness symptoms."

"Oh, congratulations."

"Thanks. I guess." I replied unenthusiastically.

"So, what happened after you collapsed?"

"I regained consciousness in an ambulance on the way to the hospital, where I was given the shocking news that I was eighteen weeks pregnant. I couldn't believe it."

"Were you happy or sad about the pregnancy?"

"A bit of both- but I think more shocked. I knew it was going to derail my plans about living in London, and I was desperate to stay there and continue my new life. Until it all became toxic over that weekend."

"What happened then?"

"Well, when I got home my cousin Rochelle, who I was staying with, started having a row with Romeo about him selling pictures of me and him together."

"Why were they rowing?"

"Because Rochelle didn't agree with Romeo selling stories, especially when he dragged me into it. But the thing is, Romeo had reasons to do it, and as much as I was pissed off that he sold them, I kind of saw where he was coming from. Although, I was crushed that he led me on."

"How did he lead you on?"

"Well…" I paused for a second:

"He's gay."

It just slipped out- I couldn't control it, it was eating away at me. I needed to tell someone, and Dr. Zoe was so easy to tell things too (even though I had only known her for the best of ten minutes).

"Please don't tell anyone." I pleaded.

"I won't. It's not my place to say." She reassured me. "Did it hurt you to find that out?"

"Yeah, I guess. I hid my sadness from him because I wanted to support him. I have friends at home who are gay, and they went through so much just because of their sexuality, and so I didn't want to see him suffer- nor did I want to be the one who caused him any suffering."

"You're a good person for doing that Nicola. But if it's having an effect on you, you have to prioritise yourself."

"But I can't- I want to be there for him. I mean I don't really know him, and I've basically ruined my relationship with Rochelle."

"How?"

"Because I said to her that she was being too harsh on him, and that I understood why he was hiding it, and why he didn't want the papers to find out. You see, the papers are after him- there are so many people who want to sell stories about his sexuality."

"Why did that cause your cousin to fall out with you?"

"Because I'm considering moving up to Newcastle with him."

"Why?"

"He made me an offer I can't really refuse: he's going to pay for me and my child to live." I paused. "But I have to pretend to the tabloids that me and him are in a relationship together."

"That's crazy. You do know that's an insane proposal, Nicola. That would likely have a hugely detrimental impact on your mental health."

"Why?"

"Because the only person who's going to gain from it, is him."

"How?"

"Look, I'm just your therapist- I shouldn't be giving you such strong advice. I'm just here to help you."

"Ok, right." I replied.

"Do you really think it's a good idea, Nicola?"

"Well, no. But someone's got to pay for this baby."

"That doesn't mean you should be forced to live a lie for a life."

"Well, I'm going to do it." I argued back.

"What else do you think is causing you to want to make this decision?"

I took a deep breath: "I had an abortion two years ago and I regret it a lot. My dad was desperate for me to get rid of the baby because we didn't have the money, and I still don't have the money right now, so I thought this was the only way I could have this baby. I want to be a mum- I know I'm young, but I've always dreamed of it."

"And why is that?"

I teared up. "Because I didn't have a mum. I wanted to give my child the love I never got growing up."

"Oh, bless you. What happened?"

"My mum left one day when I was seven and never came back. I haven't seen her since, or even heard from her. None of us have. I don't actually know what she's doing now- for all I know she could have another husband or other kids. She left us all without a word."

"Do you know why?"

"No- my dad said one day she just got up and walked out. She said her life was too stressful, and me and my brother were holding her down and not allowing her to live it."

"Do you feel like you are to blame for her leaving?"
I thought that was quite a deep question- maybe too far, but I wasn't going to start another argument with Dr. Zoe. "Yes, to be honest, I do. I wish I still had my mum, and the fact that she said she left because of me and my brother hurt a lot. It probably hurt my dad even more, because he had to quit his job and go on benefits to look after us. She gave him no help at all. She was the one with the money, but she never used to share any of it out."
"Your mum obviously had other issues going on that meant she didn't want to raise children. It was never your fault Nicola. You can't blame yourself for her leaving."
Dr. Zoe was showing a nicer side to that stone cold exterior- she was actually quite reassuring. To be honest, I didn't really know where this therapy session was going to lead, but she was really getting the information out of me. Dr. Zoe continued to write notes on a piece of paper attached to a clipboard- I wondered what problems she was going to say I had. What was the root of all the stress?
"So, do you think your mum walking out has led to events in your life becoming quite stressful?"
"I feel like I can't speak to my Dad as much because he's got the younger ones to look after - my sister and my brother. But I also think I bottle all my issues up, as does

my brother Kieran, who I think it affected as well."

"Why do you bottle it up?"

"Because I don't want to be a burden on anyone else- but I've realised how bottling it up can lead it to overflow, like it has done over the last few days."

"Can you tell me more about what actually went on after you left your cousins house?"

"I went to the train station and managed to get a train into London Victoria, but there were no trains back home, so I had to wait on a bench in Victoria, I ended up falling asleep on that bench."

"You slept on a bench?"

"Yeah, I know- it was horrible. It was one of the worst experiences of my whole life to be honest."

"Ok so what happened after that?"

"When I woke up, I was all panicked. I didn't realise I didn't have enough money to get me back home, so I only paid for a ticket to Haywards Heath. But after we passed Haywards Heath, the train guard went to check our tickets, and he found out I was bunking the fare. So, he ended up shouting at me in front of the whole train carriage, and he gave me a fine that I have to pay off soon. I don't have that kind of money to pay it off at all, and I really don't want to tell my dad. I was just desperate to get home- that's why I did it."

"I'm sure your dad would understand- sometimes we do stupid things when we're stressed. We're all human and we all make mistakes."

"Yeah, I guess."

"So, keep going, you got home?"

"When I got home, my dad wasn't expecting to see me, but I had already rung him to tell him I was pregnant, so he wanted to talk to me. I went upstairs into my room to lie down and try to escape it all. I had a nap, and when I woke up my breathing was all disjointed and messed up. I thought it would go in a few seconds, but it didn't. It kept going and it became quite fast. By the time my dad found me, I couldn't breathe. The doctors said I was having a panic attack, and that's why they referred me here."

"That's good to know. Did you want to come here?"

"No. I'd rather be anywhere else than talk about my feelings. I need to carry on with my life- I have a big decision to make."

"I think you need to talk to the people around you, and you need to do what is going to be best for my mental health."

"I understand what you're saying." I looked Dr. Zoe right in the eye.

"But I'm going to do this for my baby."

17

Walking out of the clinic, I had never felt more set on a decision in my life. Dr. Zoe had sealed it- she might have told me not to do what I was about to do, but the way she had explained everything had made me want to rebel against it all. I needed to do what was best for me and my life- the baby was going to come first, and if that meant faking a relationship with a gay footballer, I was going to do it. After all, I was already his rumoured girlfriend, and he was the fittest guy I had possibly ever seen. Actually, the second fittest after Joel.

I stepped into dad's car, and stared straight forward, saying nothing. The car journey was tense- I was completely silent. He didn't even try to talk to me. You could have cut the tension with a knife. I didn't know whether Dr. Zoe had told him about everything I said, because he was being weirdly off with me - but then again, I'm pretty sure she would be breaking the law if she had actually told my dad about everything. I think that would be wrong to do- I'm an adult at the end of the day and I'm capable of making my own decisions.

"So. How did it go?" He finally broke the silence.
"It was alright, I found it a bit awkward at times. She was

quite a confrontational lady."

"Really? I'm not sure she should be confrontational; she's there to help you."

"Well, I don't need any help." I snapped back. I was annoyed. I was fed up with people treating me like I was sick or that I had lost the plot. I hadn't, I was fine.

"Alright, Alright. You don't need to snap. I'm your dad, I'm doing something for you that I thought would be helpful, and just like that you threw it back in my face."

"I am not throwing it back in your face, I just don't want everyone to think I'm sick or crazy. Because I'm just fine. I'm going up to Newcastle, I don't know when, but I'm going to move up there."

"Oh, for fucks sake, Nicola you are driving me insane. You're so irrational sometimes- why the hell would you be moving to Newcastle?"

"To get away from everyone. I have an offer I couldn't refuse." I looked at him, he didn't turn to look at me. Instead, he screeched into a layby on the side of the road.

"Why are you so dramatic? Your life isn't crumbling in front of you. We're trying to help you; I've raised you on my own and you're going to abandon me just like that?"

"I'm not abandoning you- I don't have a choice."

"Why? Tell me why."

"It will pay for the baby."

"Will it now? What are you going to do that will pay for the baby?"

"You're just going to shout at me."

"Oh god. You better not be doing Page 3. Come on Nicola, you're classier than that."

"How would I do Page 3- I'm pregnant? They'll never take me on if I'm almost halfway along."

"Oh yeah." He rolled his eyes. "You have a point."

I didn't have the energy to hide it anymore:

"I'm going to be faking a relationship with a gay footballer."

"What?" He gasped. "You're crazy. Nicola, you've actually lost the plot. I've failed. I swear- you are absolutely insane."

"I'm so sorry Dad. But this is for my baby." I could feel myself beginning to tear up. "I can't live here and afford to pay for the baby, and I can't live at Rochelle's because she hates me."

"Can I take a wild guess at why Rochelle hates you?" He said to me, I stayed silent. "Because you've decided to move to Newcastle to fake a relationship with a gay footballer."

"The gay footballer is her brother-in-law"

"Nicola, you couldn't make this up. Why do you do this to yourself? What will you gain from all this drama? I genuinely think you're a lost cause. Don't come crying to me again because your life is all messed up, because I won't be there. There are so many easy ways out; you could get another termination-"

"You're never going to get me to the abortion clinic and force me to have another one. I only had the first one to please you. Something inside of me is telling me to have this baby, and I don't need your approval. I'll leave tomorrow morning."

"No, you can leave today. I don't want to see you."

"What? Where do you expect me to go?"

"Anywhere but here. I can't take it anymore. You pitch up at my door because you ran away –"

"I had to. I needed to get away, I was so stressed out."

"Nicola I'm fed up with excuses- let's just drive home. I can't even look at you."

Tears rolled down my cheeks, why was he being so harsh? I knew he wouldn't have understood my decision, but I didn't think he was going to shout at me, or even kick me out. What was I going to do? I didn't have anywhere else to go- I was practically homeless. I guess I was in this mess alone now, and I needed to get out fast. Romeo's offer was now a must. I was going to go to Newcastle, with or without my dad's approval.

As soon as I got home, I ran upstairs and repacked my silver suitcase all over again. I thought I was going to be staying in Brighton for a bit longer, but obviously not now that I'd been kicked out. I felt completely sick, my stomach hurt like hell, my breathing was really heavy- I was hyperventilating.

I quickly got my phone out and rang Romeo straight away.

'Romeo, I am going to come to Newcastle. I'm leaving today.'

'Today? It's 4pm. You won't make it up to Newcastle today, and I'm still in London. I'll send a car to come and get you, so you don't have to go on public transport. Is that alright? Are you OK?'

'Yeah, I'm fine. I don't really know what to say.'

'Why?'

'I've just had a really hard week. I'll explain it all to you when I see you. My dad won't speak to me because I'm moving up to Newcastle with you."

"Are you sure you want to do this?"

"Yes, Romeo. I'm sure. I need this, I want this for my life. I want my baby to be paid for, and I need someone to help me. I need you to be like a father to this baby.'

'I will, I promise, but are you sure you don't need more time to decide whether this is the best idea?'

'I'm sure.'

'Ok. A car will be with you in an hour.'

I hung up. This felt really real now- but it felt right. I know I had angered most of the people I had ever known, but this was going to be for me and my baby. I was sacrificing everything for my future child. I may have been twenty weeks pregnant, but I definitely felt like I wasn't twenty weeks a long. I needed to go for my gender scan soon as well.

18

"Where would you like to go?"

"Sloane Square."

I rushed into the back of the big black 7-seater car- it had blacked out windows and all black decor. It was like I was a secret agent- even the driver was dressed in all black with sunglasses. He looked in the mirror directly into my eyes.

"Hi. You alright?"

"Hi." I replied. I was trying to squash the conversation as quickly as possible.

"Why are you going to Sloane Square?"

"That's where Romeo's booked the hotel for us to stay at."

"Oh, of course. It's his favourite- it's really glamorous." He replied.

"I've not actually been to a hotel before. The only time I stayed away from home was in my Grandad's caravan in Worthing."

"Really? I don't think I've ever known anyone who hasn't been to a hotel before."

"Well, it's probably because I'm poor."

"Oh, I'm sorry, I didn't mean to be rude. Well, I mean as a driver, I don't make that much money- definitely not as much as people would expect me to make."

"Who do you drive around?"

"Do you know Danielle Atlas?"

"Oh god- she's in the papers more than Romeo is!"

"Yeah, I drove her for a bit."

"What was she like? I bet she was a right diva."

"No, she's actually really lovely- she's not much older than you. She's been in the public eye for a long, long time though." He explained.

"Oh- the media portrays her awfully."

"It only really changed recently- she used to be the nation's sweetheart."

"I used to idolise her a lot- I don't really anymore."

Danielle Atlas was the star of my generation, but recently the press had been really harsh towards her. They would write slanderous comments about her love life, or about what she was wearing. If I knew her, I would have loved to have a conversation with her about how to handle the UK media.

"She's mint, I swear. My favourite person to drive around- she's so nice."

"Who's your least favourite?"

"Your boyfriend."

"No way!"

"No, I'm joking."

"Who is it then?"

"I'm not going to tell you- I don't want you to go and tell everyone."

"Ok, that's fine, I understand. Sorry for asking." I had definitely made the conversation awkward.

"No, don't apologise- you're young, you're going to want to ask questions. I was like you when I was your age. Now

I'm forty-eight."

"Wow." The driver didn't look his age- he looked at least ten years younger.

"Oh, by the way, we're nearly at the hotel. I know you can't see it because the windows are blacked out, but we are going to be pulling up outside in just a few minutes."

"Is it nice here?"

"Oh, it's lovely- we're in the poshest part of London."

I couldn't believe I was back in London, three days after I escaped my cousin's house. It was a traumatic experience the first time, and I didn't want to have a repeat of the last few weeks again, so I wanted to make sure this trip was short and sweet.

*

The driver pulled open the door and I stepped out of the car. I looked up at my surroundings, and I immediately felt totally underdressed. I was in a grey tracksuit, and I had no makeup on. I put a grey cap over my head so that no one could see me walk into this hotel.

"What do I do?" I turned to the driver.

"Walk through those doors and go to the check in desk on the right. They should tell you what room you're supposed to be in."

"Ok, thank you."

I walked up to the hotel, which had a gold door with two men standing either side. I don't really know why.

"Shall we take your bag?"

"Um, no thank you." I looked at the man confused. Why was he offering to take my bags? He was probably a thief trying to steal my stuff, so I ignored him and continued to walk towards the hotel.

I walked up to the desk, and a man in a suit looked up at me.

"What's your name?"

"Nicola."

"And your second name."

"Mckenna."

"You're in Room 407: go through the doors on the left, and then up the stairs- it's the fourth floor." He passed me a silver key with a 407 engraved on it. "Here's your key- that's how you'll get in and out."

"Thank you."

I walked through the doors on the left, and then up the stairs. The stairs felt like they were never ending, and I lugged the suitcase up them, bumping it around as it hit each step one by one. I was kind of wishing I had taken that offer from the guy at the front- but I mean I didn't want my clothes stolen.

I pushed the key through the door of Room 407, and entered the room, locking the door behind me. The room was gorgeous- I couldn't believe Romeo had booked this for me to stay in. There was a massive sofa with a television, and doors to a bedroom on either side. I walked into the bedroom on the left. I gasped.

147

"Romeo? I wasn't expecting you to be here."

"Surprise!"

"How long have you been staying here?"

"Since Tuesday morning- Rochelle kicked me out after you left."

"Was she mad?" I knew what he was going to reply, but I really wanted to know how she'd reacted.

"Livid- I've never seen her that angry. But it doesn't matter. Andre didn't really mind- I think he understood to be honest. Life was getting quite stressful for you by that point."

"I had to go, but now I'm ready. I'm ready to move up north with you. Well, I have no other option- my dad kicked me out."

"We'll leave tomorrow morning- a car will come and get us and drive us up there."

"You've paid for a car to drive us all the way to Newcastle?" I still had no idea where Newcastle was, but I assumed it was quite far away from the reaction Dad had given me.

"I have a full-time driver."

"Sorry?"

"I employ a driver who drives me around full time."

"But you didn't have one at Rochelle and Andre's? You got public transport."

"Yeah, that's because my driver took time off when I got injured. And I needed to be disguised."

I looked straight at Romeo- I was stunned. How could someone have a personal driver that takes them everywhere?

"What else have you got to tell me?" I was waiting for more bombshells to come out of his mouth.

"I have a chef, and a cleaner who lives with me. My PA lives with me too."

"What is a PA?"

"Personal Assistant."

"Oh right. Got you. Why do you need a personal assistant to live with you?"

"He deals with all my business- if someone calls me or needs me, he sorts it out. He's a bit like a secretary."

"So he just does all the work you don't want to do?"

"Yep."

"You're so lazy! I cannot believe that."

"Well- we'll get you one as well."

"No way. I don't need it. Thanks for the offer though." I laughed. "I need to unpack my stuff. I'll come back in a second."

I walked into the bedroom- it was gorgeous. There was a four-poster bed which was massive- the beams were wooden, so it looked quite old fashioned, but I quite liked it. There was a large TV mounted to the wall, and on the left there was a large feature window, with ivy wrapped around the corner.

I started throwing my clothes that I usually wore for bed out of the case, trying to make sure the other clothes didn't come out with them. My suitcase was so messy- I wasn't very good at folding or being tidy. I had white shorts and a black top that I always wore for bed; I liked being cold in bed- it was much better than being sweaty. I know that might sound weird, but it was just my preference. This bed had a very thick duvet which was already bugging me, and I hadn't even gotten in the bed. But at this point I needed to count my blessings- a few hours ago I was homeless.

The door swung open, and Romeo walked in.
"Do you want to go for dinner?"
"I don't have anything to wear. Does this mean we have to do press shots?"
"I'll give you the money from them, I promise."
"How much do they pay?"
"Seven to ten thousand."
"No way? I don't believe you."
"I'm deadly serious."
"Just because we're going for dinner- how?"
"Second date. It slowly drops off from here until something bigger happens, but I'll give you 10 thousand."
"Ok fine, I'll do it. I need the money." I couldn't believe I was saying that, but what he was suggesting was a good idea, that would fund me and the baby for a couple of months. What was the big interest in Romeo? There must have been something I was missing- what was all the fuss about?

"Romeo, I've got a question."

"Hit me."

"Why is there such a huge interest in your name? That's not normal to be getting that much money for pap shots. I'm sorry to ask, but it's weird."

"Yeah I know, I never used to. Until the marriage split."

I had completely forgotten that he'd been married. It made me wonder if his ex-wife knew his secret- it's probably why she moved to America with the kids. I don't blame her to be honest; it must have been stressful with two young children, but it also meant Romeo hadn't had any contact with his children.

"Do you like the media attention?"

"Yes and no. I like it when I organise it, but when I don't plan it, or when I'm going through a tough time, I basically get stalked."

"Stalked?" I panicked - what was I getting myself into?

"Yeah, the cameramen used to follow me around, like properly chase me. It was quite stressful."

"I can imagine- I would have completely hated that."

"I'll make sure you're not stalked, I promise."

"Ok, thank you."

"Do you want to head down for dinner? The photographer is downstairs by the entrance of the hotel."

"Does he work for a newspaper?"

"No, it's a gossip magazine- we'll be in next week's issue. Splashed on the front cover, I presume."

Great, I thought. Yet another time I was going to be on the front page of something. At least this time I was making money from it, and it wasn't going to be behind my back.

Romeo pointed beside me: "Open the cupboard, the stylist has left some clothes for you to try. Trust me, they'll be good- she used to style my ex-wife"
I opened the cupboard and picked out a red dress, and quickly ran into the bathroom to put it on.
"You look so good." Romeo stated.
"Thank you. Can I quickly check my makeup?"
"Of course. We can wait until you're ready."

I dashed into my room, taking a glance in the mirror. I fixed my hair to make sure it was as straight as possible. Despite wearing this tight dress, you could barely see my bump.

"I'm here." I shouted as I walked back towards the door.
"Cool." Romeo replied. He was wearing an all-black suit- and to be honest, he looked so hot. He was quite slim; I hadn't noticed until he'd put this suit on.

He opened the door. "After you."
"What a gentleman you are!" I replied laughing. He smiled back.
He shut the door behind us and locked it. We walked towards the stairs at what I would call a quick pace, as he headed straight for the lift.

"Shall we not use the stairs?"

"The lift is easier."

"Aren't you supposed to be a footballer?"

"Yeah, and? The lift is there. I'm going to use it."

I rolled my eyes in disapproval- even I wasn't that lazy. Romeo was baffling me more and more every day- I couldn't work him out. A gay footballer, it was practically unheard of - although I presumed that was because he wouldn't have been accepted by the public, especially by football fans who were notoriously homophobic. Although he was a footballer, he was also one of the laziest I had ever come across- I don't know how he was one of the best in the country at all. He's injured, I'll give him that, but he shouldn't be taking a lift, or getting everyone else around him to do everything he needs to do. I didn't get it at all.

We stepped out of the hotel doors. Romeo nodded at those same men that I had seen standing outside the hotel offering to take my suitcase. Why was he nodding? I really didn't get it. They were thieves. As we turned a corner, a short, slightly round guy with a bald head approached us.

"You alright Romeo?" He had an accent- it sounded quite similar to a lot of people I knew from around Brighton.

"Yeah, yeah, I'm good. This is Nicola."

"You alright Nicola?" I could see chewing gum between his teeth as he spoke to me. He was practically spitting.

"Yeah, I'm good. What's your name?" I asked.

"Andrew. But I liked to be called Andy."

"What would you like us to do, Andy?" Romeo asked.

"I just want some good pictures of you two walking the street, definitely holding hands. A kiss would be great. If I can get a kiss, you could get 15 thousand."

"Is it an exclusive?" I asked.

"Oh of course, Andy is my guy. He gets me the best cut possible."

If I'm being honest, I found it weird how Romeo was selling his own pictures to the tabloids- I really didn't understand it at all. Why was he baiting himself out completely?

"Do you get a lot of celebrities who sell pictures of themselves?"

"Everyone. How do you think they stay relevant? It's all common practice. Most celebs will say they don't sell pictures of themselves, but that's all bullshit." Andy replied.

That made me understand a bit more. Romeo wasn't crazy, and it was actually what everyone else in the industry did. I wasn't surprised- it always seemed so corrupt. I was ready to play the game though. This was for my benefit- I know I was helping Romeo out, but in reality, I was doing this for me and my baby, and no one else.

"Ok Andy, where would you like us to stand?"

"I'll take a picture like I'm walking behind you. Then we will take a couple of pictures from the front."

"Ok, perfect. Nicola, is that alright with you?"

"I suppose so. I just want the money."

"Ok sweetheart; if you stand on the left, and then Romeo stands on the right."

I positioned myself to the left, grabbed Romeo's hand and we started to walk up the street. I could see the flashes going off from the sides of my eyes. Even though they were from the back, they were still quite powerful, because I could see them even though I wasn't facing the camera.

"Perfect. Perfect. Good, keep walking guys." I could hear Andy directing us to do different things.

"Are we done yet?" I asked.

"Nearly, I just need to get a few more. Keep going."

We continued to walk until we were nearly at the end of the street. Romeo let go of my hand and stopped in his tracks.

"Andy, are you done with the pictures of the back of us?"

"Yep, all good, now can I get a picture of you two kissing each other?"

"Cool."

Romeo lent in to kiss me, and the camera's flash was going crazy- it felt like every time it was starting to dim, it would blind my eyes again. We probably had to do about eight or nine kisses before Andy was finally happy to move on to the front on pictures.

"They're all good, thank you guys. Just need to get the ones of your faces walking."

We turned a corner and crossed the road so the pictures would have different scenery.

"Nicola, can you walk on the left for me again?" He asked.

"Sure." I had no idea why he always wanted me to walk on the left. Maybe it was a better angle to get my baby bump- I genuinely didn't know. We held hands as we walked down the street. The camera was continuously snapping, it was almost non-stop. I felt my eyes trying to close, but I made sure they stayed wide open, so he didn't get bad pictures of me.

"That's all done guys. You two have been amazing."

"Thanks Andy. I'll give you a ring in about forty minutes so you can take pictures at the restaurant."

What was I hearing? Romeo wanted us to take photos at the restaurant. I couldn't believe it- I had agreed to take shots of us walking down the street together, but I wasn't expecting our date to be intruded by Andy the magazine photographer taking photos of our every move.

"That's all good, Romeo. Pleasure doing business with you." He shook his hand. "See you later, Nicola."

He walked off down the road- not sure where he went. I didn't care, I was just mad that we had to take more pictures at dinner.

"You didn't tell me we were also getting pictures done at dinner?"

"Yeah, sorry about that. The restaurant needs good publicity at the moment, and I said I'd help them out. I must've forgotten to tell you."

"It's alright. Does Andy do most of your shots?"

"Yeah, he does them all. He used to take pictures of my ex-wife as well when she was in the UK. He made a fortune off of us two. He lives in a mansion down in Bournemouth, in a place called Sandbanks. Have you ever been?"

"No, definitely not. I think I've said to you before that I rarely left Brighton as a kid. This is a completely new world to me- I don't really know what to expect."

"Andy says the papers and magazines don't know you're pregnant, but there is a magazine, the same one we have just done pictures for, that wants to do an exclusive announcing your pregnancy."

"But it's not your baby, so why would they be interested?" .

"I don't really know."

"I can't say in the interview that it's your baby. Because it's not."

He looked sadly at me. "Do you know who the father of the child is?"

"No. I don't. I have three options: Ricky, Joel or Aaron. But I don't want it to be any of them."

"Why?"

"Joel has a family of his own, Ricky is insane, and Aaron has just got into a prestigious university - he's also one of my best friends."

"So you're never going to go looking for the father?" He asked.

"Not right now, no."

"Ok, I can sort of understand why, but I think it's a bit selfish. You're depriving your child of a real father, and the father of knowing their own child."

"I'll come to that when I see what the baby looks like."

"Ok. Ok. I get your point now.

Back to the interview: will you do it?"

"Depends how much money they're offering me?"

"He said in the region of forty to fifty thousand."

"Shut the front door. You're joking?"

"No, I promise you I'm not. You're really in demand already, because you're my mysterious girlfriend."

"Mysterious fake girlfriend, I'll add." He rolled his eyes.

*

He pushed open the door to the restaurant; it had a completely different vibe to the first restaurant he had taken me to - this one was decorated in a sort of beach theme, with blue and white walls. I could tell immediately that it was a Greek restaurant. There was one exactly like it at home- I had been there a couple of times in the past year for drinks with my friends, and it had always been quite good food as well.

"I love Greek food." I blurted out.

"So do I, have you had it before?"

"Yeah, a couple of times. There's one down by the Brighton Marina- I'd definitely recommend it if you are ever in the area."

"I'll take a note of that one- we play a team in Brighton at the start of May."

"You've never mentioned this. Are they good?"

"Not on the level we are, but they're alright." He replied.

I glanced over the menu- there was so much to choose from. My usual from the restaurant in Brighton was a chicken kebab that was in a pitta type thing. It was so good, so I was going to order it at this one as well. The only thing was this restaurant was much more complicated, and was quite posh, so I didn't know if they did it.

"What would you like to order?" A girl came up to us- she must have been my age, and she had really nice curly blonde hair. I was really jealous of it, and her eyes as they were electric blue. She had a sort of radiance about her.

"Do you do, like, a chicken kebab that's in a pitta?"

"Um… yeah of course. And what would you like?" She looked right towards Romeo.

"Er… I'll have the same as her."

"And what about drinks?"

"Can we have a bottle of wine for the table?"

"Yeah, I'll just need to see some ID if that's alright."

I didn't have any ID on me, which I was panicking about. I couldn't drive so I didn't have a licence, and my passport was in the pocket of my suitcase. I was a bit stupid not bringing my ID, but I swiftly stepped in because the waitress must not have realised I was pregnant. I knew roughly that you couldn't drink while pregnant, although I must have done so for a long time before I realised I was. "Actually, I'll have a diet coke."

"Ok, perfect. And you would still like that wine Sir?"

"Yeah, here's my ID."

I looked over at the ID- it was a driving licence. I mean why does he need a driver if he can drive? The date of birth read September 18th 1974- I forgot how much older than me he was. He was born in a different decade to me for god's sake- I was born on March 25th 1981, so he was almost seven years older than me. To be honest, I was surprised the papers hadn't reported on the crazy age gap.

Within minutes of ordering, the drinks had arrived.

"Thank you." I said to the waitress.

"It's alright, enjoy."

"I've got to make a phone call." Romeo stated. I knew exactly who he was ringing- that Andy guy. I was not in the mood to be papped while eating my food, but I needed to make money.

"He'll be here in about three minutes." Romeo said as he put the phone down.

"Ok cool. He won't be here for long, will he?"

"Nah, he only needs a couple of shots of us on the date. It's all part of our couple's feature. And then we'll sort out the pregnancy feature that they're going to do- they said you can wait a couple of weeks to make up your mind, so

there's no rush to decide whether or not you're going to do it."
"Ok that's fine. I probably will do it- I need the money."

*

Andy walked into the restaurant, and the waitress guided him to our table.
"Are you enjoying dinner?" He shouted over to us.
"Yeah, are you ready to take the pictures?" Romeo replied.
"All good; give me a second- I just need to get a good angle."

I realised that the other people in the restaurant were probably wondering what the hell was going on in here- there was just this small man with a camera taking pictures of us eating dinner. It was really strange, but then again, this whole day had been weird; I had gone from being in therapy in the morning, to impulsively leaving Brighton for a second time after falling out with my dad, and going to live with Romeo. I know it all sounds insane, but I was doing this for money and nothing else- I needed it. I definitely wasn't in the right frame of mind to be having pap shots done of me, but when a five-figure sum is at stake, I had to do it. It was definitely worth it.

"Can you lift up the kebab, Nicola."
"Ok."
"Perfect, that's exactly right."

"Now can you hold up the drink and put the straw in your mouth? You don't have to drink any of it, I just need a shot of it." I did exactly what he said, even though I had no idea what the appeal was of a picture of me sipping a diet coke.

"Ok, now I need to get a picture of you two holding hands across the table." He shouted over.

I rolled my eyes. I was over all these pictures- I didn't care anymore. I just wanted Andy to get his shots and then go away.

"Alright, I'll leave you guys to it."

"See ya later Andy- ring me when you know when the feature is going to be published."

"Will do Romeo. Bye."

I let out a sigh of relief.

"You look relieved."

"I hated all that- I have never felt so uncomfortable in my life. It was so awkward; I didn't know what to do."

"You were really good- I think Andy liked you as well. I think you're going to do really well at all of this stuff."

"Thank you, is it alright if next time we go out, there are no cameras?"

"Of course. We don't have to do it all the time."

"Thank you."

"Are you alright, Nic? You looked worried."

"It's been a really horrible day- I can't believe I fell out with my dad like that. He kicked me out because I've gone off with you. The thing is, he didn't even realise that I had gone because I had to make money, and I did it for the baby. But he just wanted me to get another abortion again."

"Oh Nicola, he'll come around. He should understand."

"I know, but he just didn't. And I went to therapy this morning, and this woman just grilled me on my life choices. She said I was making a mistake going up to Newcastle."

"I don't see why it's any of her business. Shouldn't a therapist be supporting and helping you?"

"Yeah, that's what I thought- but this one was just constantly negative."

"I just can't believe how chaotic the last few weeks have been- how have they turned out like this?"

"I don't even know."

I stared right at him and realised he had lost his family. I'm pretty sure he wasn't in contact with Andre or Rochelle, and I don't really know if he speaks to his parents or not. I thought that was quite a personal thing to ask him, so I refrained from bringing it up, knowing it might hurt him.

"Well, let's just hope the next few are going to be more drama free."

"I'll cheers to that!"

19

I was woken up by the shine of the morning sun through the window. The view from my bed was gorgeous of the sunrise over London- it was like something from a film. I was living a dream, waking up in a five-star London hotel- I mean I deserved it after the horrible last few weeks I had been having. I stretched my arms out, managed to sit up, and basically rolled out of bed onto the floor. I had no idea what time it was- there was no clock in my room, so I couldn't keep track of the time. I pushed the door open to find Romeo sitting on the sofa watching the TV.

"Morning, Nic. How did you sleep?"
"Good thanks- it was the comfiest bed I think I've ever slept on. How about you? Did you have a good sleep?"
"Yeah, it was mint. How are you feeling today?" He asked.
"I'm alright- much better than yesterday. Are we going to Newcastle today?"
"Yes, yes we are. The car is coming at ten."
"What time is it now?"
"Eight thirty."
"It's quite early then- I thought it was later than that if I'm honest."
"Well, you have time to get ready and get yourself sorted."
"You're right, I do. I'll start getting ready in a minute."

"What are you watching?" I asked.

"Just the morning news, nothing really that interesting- just talking about the possibility of a rise in house prices or something. I'm not really paying attention- it's quite boring."

"Sounds like it. I don't really know much about houses or anything."

"I let my accountant sort out all my financial stuff."

"Of course you do- anything that means you don't have to do it." I knew that came out nastier than I meant, but it was true, and sometimes people need the harsh truth. At this point, Romeo needed to realise it wasn't really normal that he had all these people doing all his work.

"That was mean."

"The truth."

"Ok, fine. I get what you're saying." He chucked a cushion right at me.

"Ow! That hurt." I chucked one straight back at him. We both laughed. It was really nice that for once everything wasn't so serious, and we could just have a bit of a laugh. It felt like I wasn't able to have a laugh anymore, my new life was so insane.

"I better get ready now- I'll be back in a second."

"Cool. I might have a shower."

"Nice to know." I laughed.

I walked back into my room and started pulling clothes out of my suitcase. I settled on a white jumper, with denim jeans. It was a quite plain and basic outfit, but I was going to wear it to hide the baby bump- I could feel it getting bigger by the day. I put on the clothes quickly and walked back out into the living area. There was Romeo lying in the exact position I'd last seen him.

"So you didn't go for a shower then?"

"No, I am. I just couldn't get up, but I'll go now."

"Go quick, your car's going to be here soon."

"OK, OK. I'll be back in a second."

He got up and walked into his room, and I took his exact space on the sofa and lay there. I reached over for the remote and started flicking over the channels. It all felt like news, and more news. That was until I got to Channel 8. I used to love watching Channel 8, especially if I was off school- it was the channel for pop culture and celebrity gossip. The show that was usually on at this time was called 'Morning Run-down' and it was like a bulletin of pop news:

'Danielle Atlas seen out with mystery man after recent split from Jax Lee last month. Danielle, 19, was seen walking around a shopping centre with this man looking at watches.'

'Singer Louisa Blue is in a stable condition after a car crash- the singer was rumoured to be drunk when she got behind the wheel last Wednesday. She was found unconscious and was transported to hospital where she has remained ever since. Louisa, 28, was recently charged with drug possession as this car crash is the latest drama in her crazy life. The singer has four children, who will no doubt be affected by all of this.'

*'And finally, footballer Romeo Lomax has been spotted
with a new woman-'*

Oh, not again, I thought. Why does this always happen to
me? Why do I see myself in everything? First, I was in the
papers and now I was on the Channel 8 morning rundown.
I was so confused as to how they'd managed to get the
pictures of me and Romeo out on the date.
"ROMEO. ROMEO!"
"What?" He peered round the door.
"Why are we on the TV?"
"Oh for god's sake. Andy must have sold the pictures to
Channel 8. I thought they were for OutOut Magazine."
"Well, they're obviously not, because then they wouldn't
be on the screen."
"Don't worry about it Nikki, I'll sort it out. All it means is
we'll get more money, or less if OutOut were looking for
an exclusive photoshoot."
"Good to know." I was slightly apprehensive about the
paycheck- I didn't want it to be less than I was promised. I
think I'd have properly flipped out at seeing myself on the
screen if I hadn't known that I'd be getting enough money
to last me months in return. I barely had a penny to my
name and didn't have a bank account either.

*'The woman in question is 18-year-old Nicola Mckenna.
Nicola is rumoured to be pregnant, but not with his child.'*

My heart stopped; my body started shaking. How did they know I was pregnant? This was a disaster. All my friends were going to find out, my ex-boyfriends were going to know. I was going to have to face it all, and to top it all off I was risking losing a huge fifty-thousand-pound deal. Which I needed, because that would literally get me through years without ever having to work again.

"ROMEO! They know I'm pregnant. You didn't tip them off, did you?"

"No of course not- I wouldn't. I wouldn't want to sabotage your exclusive with the magazine. It must have been Andy. I swear to God I'm going to kill him- he's just gone and leaked everything to Channel 8, and it's bang out of order."

"Here's a solution- just don't use him next time."

"Good idea."

*

"The cars here!" Romeo shouted from the other room.

"Ok, coming." I pulled my suitcase out from the bedroom and lugged it over to the hallway.

"Do you want me to carry that?" Romeo asked.

"Yes please, it's so heavy. Where is all your stuff?"

"I took it down to the car already."

"Oh right, how long has the car been parked down there?"

"Not long, like three or four minutes."

"That's quick of you. Did you have much to take?"

"No not at all- it's already mostly in Newcastle. I still have a lot of stuff at my brother's, but I don't have the guts to go back there. Rochelle would eat me alive. I bet she's told Andre everything, and I don't really blame her either."

"They definitely both hate us. She still sends me angry hate messages to my phone, so much so that I've had to block her."

"Why is she so mean? She's quite rotten but I choose to ignore her a lot of the time. She sends me messages too. I don't really know what she thinks she's going to gain from being so horrid."

"No, I don't either- I mean I feel bad that I left in the middle of the night without any real announcement after everything that she did for me. But I had to because it was all too stressful. I felt pressure from her to cut you out and I didn't want to, I felt pressure from her to make choices in my life - one's I wasn't ready to make."

"Yeah, I totally understand. Shall we get in the car?"

We walked down the stairs of the hotel and into the lobby- it was so grand. I hadn't noticed how pretty it was when I had walked in because I had been so busy trying to avoid the thieves in front of the hotel who were patrolling. The lobby was decorated in gold with a couple of dark red walls on either side. I could see a restaurant either side of the lobby- it made me wonder why we didn't just eat in the restaurants in the hotel. It would have been so much easier. But it was Romeo's choice, and I had to accept that.

As we walked outside, I saw the same two men who were standing outside of the hotel. One of them nodded at me. I was so confused. Why hadn't the hotel done something about them and got them arrested for theft?

The same driver who drove me from Brighton was here to collect us.

"You alright Nicola?"

"Yeah, how have you been?"

"All good. Are you excited to go to Newcastle?"

"Oh definitely- I've never been up north before."

"She must like you- she's quite chatty with you." Romeo interjected.

What a strange thing to say. I did like the driver, but that was because he was one of the only people that I knew right now who didn't have a mandate or a hidden motive. He was just a genuine nice guy.

"What's our ETA to Newcastle?" Romeo asked.

"We should be there before four."

"Four? How long away is it?" I was shocked.

"About four to five hours, so we'll probably have to stop on the way."

"That's ages. I don't think I've ever been in a car for that long."

"You'll be fine. We've got loads of drinks in the back- I stocked up especially for you two."

"Thanks, Xavier."

"My pleasure Romeo." He smiled. "Let's go, shall we?"

He swung open the door, Romeo attempted to get in first.

"Wait- Romeo, do you not know the common courtesy of ladies first?"

Romeo got out of the car. He looked quite embarrassed.

"Er… Sorry Nic."

"It's alright, don't worry about it." I laughed.

I got into the car, and Romeo soon followed on. The driver shut the door, and it all became real: I was moving again.

As we left, I realised there was no turning back from this life. I was going to have to live with this choice for the rest of my life. I was going to be in the public eye- well, I already was.

"What are we going to do when we get to Newcastle?" I asked.

"Well, I'll show you around everything. And then I need to go to training tomorrow, and you can go shopping or something to distract yourself."

"Ok, will I have cameras taking pictures of me?"

"No, I can't imagine so- just don't attract any attention."

"Got you, is Newcastle good for shops?"

"Yeah, I would say so. There's a lot of the usual chain shops, especially in the town centre. I'm sure you'll like it."

"Cool."

"My house is quite near a metro station."

"What's a metro station?" I had never heard of that before.

"What. Nicola, tell me you're joking-."

"I'm not, what is it?"

"It's an underground railway station- we have one in Newcastle, and it connects the whole town up. It's much quicker than getting a bus, so it's really convenient."

"Oh right. I never knew. I didn't even realise you could get underground trains outside of London."

Romeo looked baffled, but I was being serious. I guess it was showing how I'd never really left Brighton and was quite sheltered from the world. There was a whole world out there that I had never even heard of.

"You're making me laugh so much. How did you not know there was an underground network outside of London? How do you get to the age of eighteen and not realise that?"

"I guess some people aren't as privileged as you Romeo."

"So true!" The driver piped up.

"This is actually so rude. Xavier, you better watch your mouth. I'm not the one related to royalty!"

"Related to royalty?"

"Xavier is a distant cousin of the Spanish royal family."

"Seriously?"

"Yep. I've never met them, but I know of them." Xavier added.

"That's actually so cool."

"I guess- I don't really say much about it because we've constantly got Romeo yapping on about his flashy new gear or whatever."

That made me laugh a lot, finally someone was putting Romeo in his place like he deserved. He was so arrogant and thought that he was the best. It was nice that Xavier put him down a peg.

"Oi, Xavier. Stop. You're being rude."

"It's all true." He laughed.

I didn't know how Romeo was feeling on the inside- I hoped he was taking it all as banter because I didn't want this car journey to be awkward. Romeo was very complex, and sometimes I couldn't work out what he was actually feeling.

"Haha. Xavier, where are we?" Romeo asked.

I was glad he wasn't annoyed- that must have just been what their relationship was like, a bit of a laugh.

"We've come onto the M1- we're passing Enfield right now."

"Great, thank you Xavier."

*

We pulled into a small service station called Newport Pagnell. I had never heard of it in my life. To me, this was the middle of nowhere.

"Where actually are we?"

"We've just come off the M1 near Milton Keynes."

"Where's that?"

"I'll see if there's a map in the service station to show you."

I can't lie, my geography skills weren't great- I gave it up before GCSEs. I knew where London was, and what towns were on the south coast, but that was about it.

That's where my knowledge of the towns of the UK stopped.

We walked into a building with a sign saying, 'Welcome Break'. It was quite drab, and ugly. And really busy. I had never seen so many people in my life in one place. People were quite literally running from either end of the building, into each restaurant. There were tables littered around the hall- it was massive. I rushed in and out of the toilet speedily to make sure I was out of Newport Pagnell as quickly as possible. I would easily compare it to what I imagine hell to be like. It was horrific.

Romeo and Xavier were waiting outside of the car for me, and I rushed straight back into my seat without saying a word.

"You weren't a fan of that were you?"

"It was horrible- there were so many people. I hate large crowds. They are my biggest fear, especially as I'm pregnant."

"Yeah, I understand, but all service stations are like that. They don't get any better."

"Well that's great to know. The toilets were disgusting- they hadn't been cleaned at all. Oh, it was all just disgusting."

"You're secretly such a snob, aren't you?"

"Yeah maybe- I'm a working-class girl through and through and even I can't take that."

*

"Are we nearly there?"

"Yes, we're actually only ten minutes away from Romeo's house." Xavier replied.

Thank God, I thought, this had been the longest car journey ever. It was almost 4pm and we'd left London just after 10am. I felt as if I was glued to my seat- it was a weird feeling. I was fed up with sitting down, and it was getting really uncomfortable, especially with the bump. I didn't like it all.

"This is Newcastle." Romeo said.

I looked straight out of the window- there were a lot of terraced houses, all painted red. They were quite similar to the houses that were near my house in Hove. They weren't glamorous at all, but I actually quite liked the look of Newcastle.

"How long have you lived here?" I asked Romeo.

"Just under three years- I transferred in the Summer of 1997."

"The highest transfer for a midfielder in the UK at the time, I'd like to add." Xavier added.

"Really? How much?"

"Two million."

"No way!"

"Yep. It was a lot of pressure- I had been playing in Italy before that, at a club in Milan."

"That's quite cool. Did you like playing in Milan? Sorry I'm bombarding you with questions."

"It's alright, it's making the time go quicker. Yeah, if I'm being honest, I much preferred playing in Milan to playing here in Newcastle. For one, when I was in Milan, no one bothered me."

"We're here!" Xavier announced.
"Thank god." I was so relieved. I looked out of the window at Romeo's house- my eyes felt like they popped out of their sockets. "It's so big. It's like a mansion!"
"It definitely is a mansion." Xavier agreed.
"It's gorgeous. Romeo, you're actually minted."
"I guess. Shall we go inside?"
"Yes please!"
Xavier got out of the car and opened the boot. I stepped out of the car- my legs felt like jelly because I hadn't moved them since we'd stopped off at that dreadful service station.
"Thanks, Xavier." He passed my suitcase over to me. "I'll see you soon."
"See you soon, Nicola."

Romeo pressed a button on the left wall, which opened the gates to the house. There was a long winding driveway up to the house, with three cars parked on the top. They all had blacked out windows, which I thought was quite cool, and fun paint jobs: one was red, one was purple, and one was white.
"I've never seen a house like it."
"I am quite proud of this- I would say it's my most prized possession. It's the thing I'm most scared about losing if I lose my contract or something."

"How much do you have to pay for a house like this?"

"A million, maybe a bit more. It took me a long time to save enough money for this- I lived in a box in the town centre for a long time."

Romeo put his key into the front door, and we entered the mansion. It had not one but two staircases in the entrance hall. It was decorated all in white and had striking similarities to the decor of Rochelle's and Andre's house.

"I don't mean to be rude, but it kind of reminds me of Rochelle and Andre's."

"That's not rude- we used the same interior designer, so she basically designed the houses the same. I know it looks like I must've copied them, but in reality, they copied me."

"Oh right. No, I like the house. It's very grand- maybe a bit big for one person though."

"Well, my ex and the kids used to live here."

"Oh, sorry- I shouldn't have mentioned it." I felt really guilty- I knew how much he missed his kids. I could totally see why he would- they were all the way in America. I don't know why he didn't fight to see them- he seemed to just accept it.

"No, it's alright. Don't worry." He gestured to the stairs. "I'll show you to your room."

"Thank you."

We walked up the stairs, and I followed Romeo as he turned left along the corridor. The corridor was very long- I think we must have passed about five doors on the way to my room. He opened the door at the end, and I looked in. I was in awe- the room was even bigger than the hotel room I'd stayed in.

"Oh my god, Romeo. It's so big. It's so nice!" I looked around the room, it had a walk-in wardrobe and a massive feature window overlooking a really long garden.

"Your garden is so big." I pointed outside. "And so well kept."

"I actually love gardening- you might be surprised. It's my biggest passion outside of football. I spend most Sundays out there."

"Do you not go out on a Sunday?"

"I don't have that many friends. I'm kind of a loner really."

"What do you do in the garden?"

"I just try and grow all different types of things. And I try to keep it nice- it looks nicer in the summer when everything flowers."

"I don't really have a garden at home- it's just like a slab of concrete." I replied. No one in Brighton really had any form of garden, because our houses were all built so close to each other. My garden was just rotting away- my dad rarely ever touched it.

"Do you want me to leave you to it? The bathroom is on the right." Romeo said.

"Yeah sure, I'll be down in a few minutes."

Romeo left the room, leaving the door ajar. I collapsed onto my new double bed. It was the comfiest bed I'd ever been on in my life. My head was sinking into the pillow.

This was my new life: I was starting all over again.

20

A thud on the door.

"Oh sorry, sorry. I'll leave you to sleep."

All I could see out of my weary eyes was this woman standing by my bed. She had a set of cleaning tools.

"No, no. It's fine." I replied. "Are you cleaning?"

"Yeah, Romeo sent me up here."

"Don't worry about my room- it's fine. I'll be able to clean it myself."

"No, I have to. It's part of my job."

"No, please don't worry. I don't want you doing my work."

"Are you sure?"

"Yeah, 100%, what's your name?"

"Nadia. What's yours?"

"Nicola."

"Are you Romeo's friend?"

"Yeah, I guess. I think friend is quite a strong word."

"Well, he seems to think the world of you- he hasn't shut up about you since you both got here."

"Really?" I was confused, why was he talking about me so much?

"Yeah, he says you've saved him."

That was true- otherwise the papers would have outed him. I mean, as much as he was doing me a big favour, I was doing him a bigger favour- if it wasn't for me, he would lose everything.

"Oh wow, I don't think that's true, but he's a nice guy."

"He really is- he's my favourite person I've ever worked for."

"How long have you been a cleaner for?"

"Since I was fourteen, so fifteen years."

"Do you like it?"

"It's not what I'd seen myself doing, but I had to. I came from Argentina when I was really young, and I didn't have any skills, so I went to work with my mum who worked as a cleaner for some very rich people."

"What would you want to do if you could do something else?"

"I wanted to be a dancer, but I hurt myself." She pointed to a small white bandage around her ankle. "Cleaning accident, about five years ago. It never recovered."

"Oh no- I'm so sorry Nadia."

"It's alright - I've come to terms with it now. So why are you here with Romeo?" She looked towards me, "If you don't mind me asking?"

"Oh, it's alright, I'm just here as his friend. He's going to help me launch a career in glamour modelling, but obviously not at the moment because, you know."

"Why?"

"I'm pregnant."

"Really? I wouldn't have been able to tell. Your bump isn't very big."

"Yeah, it isn't really very noticeable."

"I best get cleaning the rest of the house."
"See you later, Nadia."

I kept thinking about Nadia and what she'd been saying to me, and I was really intrigued about how she had ended up cleaning for Romeo.

I got out of bed, and in and out of the shower. I was always quite quick when going in the shower, but this one was really fancy - no shock there. All of Romeo's house was fancy - I mean every single last bit was. The bathroom was all made of marble, with a massive bath in the centre. I'd say it was bigger than my actual bedroom at home. It was huge- I'd never known a bathroom to have two sinks.

I rushed out of the bathroom and checked the time. I breathed a sigh of relief when I saw it was just before nine- I had lots of time to get ready. I looked in my wardrobe- it looked quite empty. I definitely needed to go clothes shopping; I was going to need to go today, otherwise I'd run out of outfits by the end of the week.

I went with the same kind of outfit I was used to, a denim jacket with a white top. I mean it was basic, but I didn't want to attract any attention. The outfit showed my bump a little more than other outfits had, but I liked it. I walked down the stairs and into Romeo's kitchen. When I say kitchen, it was multiple rooms. It was massive- I had never seen anything like it. To my surprise, Romeo was sitting on the bar stools next to the island, while a man and a woman I'd never seen before were sitting at the table.

"Nicola, you alright?" He asked.

"Yeah, I'm good."

"This is Jamie, he's one of my teammates, and this is his wife, Paige."

Paige ran up to hug me. She had long blonde extensions, and eyelashes on. I recognised her from somewhere- I think she was on a show not too long ago.

"Hi Nicola. How are you?"

"I'm good, how are you Paige?"

"I'm great- while the boys go to training today, us girls are going to go shopping!"

"Oh that's perfect, I need some new clothes."

"Amazing- we'll head out in a little bit, my cars parked outside."

Jamie went up to give me a hug as well. But he didn't speak as much- I got just a nod from him.

"Nikki, do you want some breakfast? We have some pancakes." He passed me a plate with one on it.

I sat beside Paige, who smiled at me. I couldn't work out how old she was, but I presumed she was at least a few years older than me, because she was married. I noticed the big rock on her finger immediately. God knows how much Jamie spent on that. She was also dressed in designer gear- literally everything she was wearing was designer. Her sunglasses were on the table, and she had a phone with a diamond decorated phone case. Her nails were painted in a cream colour- definitely acrylic.

*

As I went to grab my bag and phone ready to go out, Romeo pulled me into a spare bedroom.

"Are you alright going with Paige?"

"Yeah of course, I needed clothes- my wardrobe is lacking." I replied.

"The main reason I wanted you two to meet is because she's been in this industry for ages, and she's been in the footballer's wife clique for a long time."

"Is she a prominent figure in it?"

"Yes, but she's the nicest one. And Jamie is my best friend. If you have any questions, please ask her- she knows this world inside out."

"Has she got any children?"

"Yeah, she's got two. One is five and the other is three, so you can ask her about all that as well."

"Oh good- I'll take any advice I can get."

"You're going to have a great time- Paige is great. Oh, and before I forget." He reached for his pocket, and pulled out a bunch of notes, wrapped in an elastic band. "Here's 1000. In case you need anything."

"Oh, Romeo, that's not necessary."

"Take it as a thank you."

"I don't need all this money."

"No, take it. Get yourself some nice clothes."

"Romeo, you're amazing."

We both walked downstairs, and Paige and Jamie were standing in the hallway.

"Nicola, are you ready?"

"Ready to hit the shops!"

"I'll see you later Romeo." I gave him a hug. "Bye Jamie."

"Nice meeting you, Nicola." Jamie replied.

Paige opened the door, and we walked towards her car. Her car was massive- it was the same make as the car that the driver had had, but white.

"I love your car, Paige!"

"Aw thank you, do you have a car?"

"No, I can't drive- I used to learn but I failed my test three times."

"Oh, don't worry about it, it took me seven attempts to pass!"

"That makes me feel a bit better." I laughed.

"Good - one day you'll pass, I promise. You've got to get Romeo to enrol you in lessons up here."

"Yeah, I might start up again, but Romeo seems to just call the driver when he needs to be picked up."

"Oh my god, I know. He's so lazy- but I mean he has the money for it. Jamie is quite different in that way; he won't let anyone else do work for him. And Jamie loves driving - most of our money goes on his cars, or my surgery."

"Surgery?"

"I've got my breasts done twice, and I get my lips done quite often."

"You look really good, you're stunning!" I was desperate to get in her good books, because she scared me a little bit.

"That's very kind Nicola- so are you."

After that conversation, the car was filled with silence. She had the radio on, but even then, it still felt awkward.

"So, Nicola. Romeo says you want to be a glamour model."

"Yes, it's been my dream for a long time- obviously I can't because I'm pregnant at the moment."

"I was a glamour model too, before I had my first. I was in the papers, on page 3 every week for a good two years. When I fell pregnant, I quit because I didn't need to do it anymore, but I went back recently. One of the magazines called it my comeback, and I did a TV appearance on a singing show a couple of months back."

"Oh I saw that, was it Celebrity Showdown?"

"Yeah! I really enjoyed myself on that show, it was a lot of fun."

"I voted for you on it." That was a complete lie, but I was desperate to impress her.

"Aw thank you! You're such a sweetheart, I was a bit upset when I got knocked out, but I mean I knew I wasn't the best singer on it." She smiled.

"So why did you choose to help Romeo? I'm really intrigued."

"What do you mean help out?"

"You know what I mean- hiding his sexuality."

"Oh it's a really long story- but I met him because his brother is married to my cousin, and we hit it off straight away, and then there was an incident with the papers, and that's why he revealed to me about his sexuality, and it really hit home because I have friends who are gay at home, and I know what they go through. Oh, and Romeo offered me a deal I couldn't refuse."

"What was the deal?"

"He said he'd help launch my career, while also paying for the baby. But the pap shots we've already done have made nearly enough money for me to live comfortably for the next two years on my own."

"Good! I'm glad- Romeo's a nice guy- I think he's quite misunderstood a lot of the time, but I really like him. Also, we've got to be quiet about the whole gay thing around Jamie. I don't think he knows- Romeo doesn't want any of the team knowing."

"That's fair enough- he knows my lips are sealed. How did you find out?"

"My brother's gay, and he's out. So, Romeo came to me for advice one day, and I gave it to him. I feel for Romeo- if it gets out, he could lose everything, and there are a lot of people out there to destroy him. Like Pandora."

"I heard about Pandora- she was friends with my cousin."

"Oh, she's rotten. She is the ice witch; I'm telling you now."

"Oh? I was going to meet her before I left- I have her number."

"Do me a favour: delete it. She's a nasty piece of work. She makes up lies constantly- she told everyone in the industry that she was dating Romeo, but that wasn't even true."

"Really? My cousin said they were an item for quite a while."

"All a load of bullshit. I'm telling you, I met her once when she tried to get press shots of her watching Romeo at the football. I told her to leave, but she refused. She's horrible- and she plays it in the media like she was messed up by her relationship with Romeo, when in actual fact she was just a messed-up stalker."

"Oh gross, I am glad I didn't call her! She sounds horrible."

"She is. Avoid at all costs."

*

After parking the car, we walked towards the metro centre.

"Have you ever been here before?" Paige asked.

"No, I haven't."

"It's my favourite place to go shopping- you won't find anything else on this level around here. I do like the shopping centre in Gateshead though, but I forgot the name of it." She pointed towards a large clothes shop- it looked quite posh. "Let's go in here."

"Ok!" I followed.

Immediately after walking in, Paige was throwing things into her basket. She wasn't even looking at prices or sizes. At this rate, there wasn't going to be anything left in the shop- she had literally got every dress, every jacket, every colour.

We walked around every shop in that centre, and by the time we left the last one I had more bags than I could possibly carry.

"Do you want to go sit in a cafe?" Paige asked.

"Yeah of course. Do you know if there's any near."

"Yeah, there's one round the corner."

I dragged my bags along as I followed Paige to the cafe-somehow, she had less bags than I did, which was crazy considering how many clothes she had bought.

The cafe itself was quite small, but it was all flashy and new. It was decorated in very neutral colours, and was very clean. It was definitely much cleaner than the usual cafes I was going into, but it was also decorated much nicer.

"Would you like coffee?" Paige asked.

"No, I'm alright thank you- can I have some water please?"

"Yeah of course, I'll get you a bottle. Do you want to find us a place to sit upstairs?"

"Yes!"

I could barely fit my bags through the narrow staircase leading to the upstairs seating. I sat down on a four-seater with a table to make sure I had enough room to put all my bags around me. I sat looking around the cafe- it was pretty empty except for a few workers dressed in business clothes with portable computers. I rarely saw people with these portable computers, but I was fascinated by the fact you could take them wherever. I didn't know anyone who actually owned one, I just saw businesspeople carry them around. They did look heavy though- I don't think I would have wanted to carry one around the metro centre.

Paige came up to drop off all her bags before going to collect the drinks from downstairs. She came back upstairs and sat down opposite me.
"I've had fun today." She said.
"So have I- it's been really good getting to know you." I replied.
"You're a really lovely girl- I think you're going to fit in well around here. We'll have to organise a little get together with the other girls from the football club. Are you going to be at the game on Sunday?"
"Maybe? I'm not sure. I need to ask Romeo if he wants me to come."
"I'm sure he will- it will be good for you to get to know the girls, and also to see Romeo play. And I'm going to be honest because Jamie's not here; Romeo is definitely the best player on the team. That's why he's got such a big contract."
"He's definitely not humble about it either- he's always flaunting his money."

"Tell me about it- Jamie is the same. But now we're making similar money, his money mainly goes on the house and the assets, while my money goes on the kids. I have to pay fifty thousand a year in school fees."

"Fifty thousand? I thought school was free."

"Nicola, tell me you've heard of private school?"

"No, what is that?"

"It's like a prestigious school you pay to go to. Jamie had his heart set on sending both of them going- I was unbothered either way."

I thought for a minute; I didn't realise people paid to go to school- I thought everyone went to school for free. Everyone who had lived around me had gone to normal schools- at least that I was aware of. I didn't know of any fancy schools in the area.

"Have you got any advice on the baby? What do I need to do?" I asked. I was in a right panic about it all.

"You don't need to worry- I think you'll be a great mum. The only tip I have is to try and get as much sleep as possible before the baby comes along."

"Ok thank you, what are yours called?"

"I have Jet who is five, and Angel is three."

"I like those names."

"Well, Angel is badly named because she is definitely not an Angel. That kid drives me insane- it's just because of the age she is, I think. Before she was good as gold, so I'm hoping it's a phase."

"I'm sure it is; my brother Carter was a nightmare when he was three. Now he's four and he's a bit better. I mean he still has his moments, but he was recently diagnosed with ADHD."

"That's quite early to get a diagnosis, isn't it?"

"Yeah, we knew from when he was really young, so my dad got him checked out as soon as possible and we were right."

"That's interesting- my brother has ADHD as well. He's twenty-eight now but he was diagnosed when he was six or seven."

I sat there sipping my water, looking at all my bags of shopping. I didn't really know what to do with it all- I'd nearly blown all the money Romeo had given me and I was quite embarrassed that I'd let myself spend so much.

"I can't believe I've bought all these clothes. I've spent way too much."

"I wouldn't say that- that's tame compared to what I've bought."

Paige was right, she had spent a lot more than I had, but that was from her own money- I had spent someone else's. I knew Romeo wanted me to get some clothes, but I don't know how he was going to react when all I was going to be handing him back was a single twenty-pound note.

"Don't worry, Romeo's not going to be mad." Paige tried to reassure me.

I didn't think he'd be angry; I think he'd just be shocked about how much money I had spent.

Paige pulled into the driveway of Romeo's house, and I could see him waving from the front door.

"How do I tell him?"

"He won't mind- he'll be happy you've got some new clothes. Especially if you're going to have to be doing more press shots."

"He organised a shoot to announce my pregnancy in a magazine."

"Do you want that?"

"Yeah, I guess- they've offered me a lot of money."

"I bet they have- you're in demand at the moment. Just be careful for me please. This world can be a bit dangerous."

I stopped for a second and thought: what did she mean? What was she talking about? I knew the world of the tabloids was toxic, but what was she warning me of?

"Thanks so much for today- I'll see you soon, yeah?"

"Yeah of course, come and see me on Sunday."

"Ok I will. Bye!"

"Bye Nicola!"

I stepped out of the car and waved behind me to Paige. She waved back and drove off.

"You alright Nic? You've got a lot of shopping there."

"I might have gone a bit crazy. I spent all of the money."

"That's alright, I'm glad you did."

"I thought you'd be mad…"

"No, how could I be? It's only a thousand."

"Only? It's a lot of money."

"Well, you didn't seem to have any issue with spending it so quickly." He laughed.

He wasn't wrong- it had taken me a matter of hours to spend all of that money. But he seemed to be seeing the funny side of it, and definitely didn't look mad.

"I needed clothes though. I was in a desperate need." I replied.

"Yeah I know, that's why I gave you the money. Shall we go inside now, I'm really cold."

"Of course"

"What would you like for dinner?"

"I don't mind, what do you want?" I replied.

"I think I fancy some pasta- I'll need to go and buy some from the shop in a bit."

"Ok that's good with me, I like pasta."

I walked up the stairs and back into my room. I could hear Romeo crashing around downstairs in the kitchen- I knew for a fact he wasn't going to be a very good cook. I started to unpack my bags and put all my clothes into the wardrobe. One after the other, I hung them up next to each other, and the wardrobe was filling up quickly- it was basically full after I had put the last jacket in. I closed the door and lay on my bed, wondering what Paige meant by being careful. Was she saying that there was something out there? What did she mean? I was panicking by this point, but I forced myself to believe it was all just an overreaction, and she was just looking out for me because she knew the industry. I tried to tell myself not to panic, but it was hard.

"I'll be twenty minutes Nic- I'm just popping to the shops." Romeo shouted up the stairs.
"Ok, see you in a bit." I shouted back.
The door shut, and everything was silent. I was alone- no one was in the house but me. It was quite creepy because it was such a big house, and it felt even bigger when no one else was in it. I walked downstairs to see what else was in the house. I wanted to explore- there was so much I hadn't seen.

I walked into the kitchen- it was dark, so I switched the light on. I gasped. I couldn't move.
I could see three men in the garden.
They were dressed in all black and had bandanas around their heads. I was frozen. I could see one of them stare right into me. They were walking towards me- only the glass doors were separating them from me. What were they doing? I was in complete shock and fear - I couldn't stop shaking no matter how hard I tried.

The tallest one ran straight to the window, grabbed what I think was a hammer out of his bag and plunged it into the glass. I ran back as it shattered, sharp shards being thrown straight towards me. I felt one hit my face and could feel blood beginning to trickle down my forehead. The men ran through the broken glass door towards me. The

shortest one ran straight past me into the house, but the other two men headed straight towards me. The man on the left reached for his pocket and pulled out what I think was a machete. He started waving it at me. I screamed- I was terrified. I was completely trapped.
"HELP. HELP. HELP. SOMEBODY, PLEASE!"

"Shut up." His knife edged closer to me. "Put the cuffs on her."
"No." I shouted.
"Do it, or we'll knife you." He threatened, the blade of the knife making contact with my skin.
Suddenly, they had my hands tied behind me with a rope, and my mouth bound by a piece of cloth.
"H-help." My voice was completely muffled.
The two men ran off, leaving me bleeding. They were carrying large black bags and were throwing items into them. I watched as they took everything they could in the kitchen, before they moved onto the other rooms. I could hear them smashing everything up- there was nothing I could do. I was helpless, and the blood just kept flowing- I could see it dripping down past my cheek and onto my clothes.

I could hear crashing upstairs as they ran through the house. My brain was in shutdown- I had no idea what to do. I had never experienced anything like this. Why did it have to happen when everyone was out of the house, and I was completely alone? I was terrified. I tried to scream, but the cloth was tied so tightly I could barely breathe. I winced in pain as I could feel the cut on my forehead. My vision was completely blurred - it felt as if my whole body was covered in blood.

I heard the key go through the door- I was hoping with any energy left in me that it was Romeo. I was praying it was Romeo.
"What the fuck has gone on here?" Thank God - he was back. I breathed a sigh of relief. "Where has all my stuff gone? It's all gone."
I could hear his footsteps advancing towards me. Meanwhile, the crashing around upstairs had completely stopped- it was silent.

He came running into the room.
"Oh my god. Nicola? What happened? We need to get you to the hospital now." He started untying me and took the cloth off my mouth. "Get in my car."
"But what about the rest of the house? I think they're still in here." I gasped out.
"It doesn't matter right now- we need to make sure you're safe. I'm about to ring Jamie, he'll be here in five minutes."

Romeo rushed me out of the door and into the car. I looked in the wing mirror and gasped in shock. I was still bleeding- it was much worse than I even imagined. I was speechless. I was just hoping I wasn't losing too much blood.

Jamie was running towards the front door- I saw the panic in his face as he rushed in. Romeo ran into the driver's seat of the car. He fastened his seatbelt, and pushed on the pedal with a lot of aggression. He looked upset, angry and scared. He was just as shocked as I was.

As we reversed out of the drive, I could hear sirens coming down the road- we were the only house on the street, so I knew exactly where they were going. Romeo unwound his window and shouted out at them:
"Officer, my friend Jamie is there- he's going to stay there until I get back. We were broken into."
"Ok, we'll do our best" The police drove straight past us and towards the house.

An awkward silence followed before Romeo opened his mouth,
"What- what actually happened?" He asked me, after he finally calmed himself down.
"Well, there were three men in bandanas – they got into the garden – smashed up the doors." I tried to explain, but I could barely form sentences with all the pain.
"What? How did they get into the garden... Nicola, did they take anything?"

"I don't know. I heard them upstairs but as soon as you walked in they were gone. How long? Please, I need help now" I cried out.

"It's alright, we're nearly there- only five minutes away. Don't touch it. You'll be OK, I promise."

I sat there, staring at the never-ending road. Where was this hospital? Blood was blocking my vision, so I couldn't actually see much of the surroundings. I could barely see Romeo driving as I turned to face him. From what I could make out, he looked very stressed.

*

Romeo forced open the car door and picked me up from out of my seat. By this point, my eyes were starting to shut. My body was slowly going numb- I felt as if my limbs were about to fall off. I could hear voices around me, but I could barely make out what they were saying. I could feel myself being thrown onto what felt like a bed. My head was squished into a pillow, and I could hear people screaming.

I drifted off to sleep, losing the noise of everyone around me.

21

I felt my eyes slowly open- I was blinded by the bright
fluorescent lights above me. I could hear a voice from the
background.
"Nicola? Nic? Are you awake?"
I didn't know who it was, or how to answer back. I
continued to stare at the lights.
"SOMEONE GET A DOCTOR." I heard someone shout.

"She's awake, she's awake."

"I can see her eyes open."

"Ok, I'll run some tests to see how she is. This is
miraculous- I didn't think she'd come around so quickly.
Nicola, are you with us? Can you hear me?"
I tilted my head up and down ever so slightly in a
desperate attempt to communicate- I needed them to
realise I was awake, but I couldn't speak.

I had no idea what had happened, or what was going on.
All I could remember was glass being shattered
everywhere at Romeo's house, the rest was a blur. I think I
was tied up by some intruders in the house. I could still
feel the marks around my wrists.
I felt as if I was a prisoner. I was trapped in this life. A
fake life.

22

"Nic, Nicola. Are you awake?"

My eyes opened slightly- I could just about make out a figure. It was my dad, looking down at me with tears in his eyes.

"Dad?"

"I'm here, what happened?"

"I-I don't know. I really don't know. I can't remember, I wish I could, but I can't."

"It's fine Nic - no one expects you to remember what happened. You probably went into shock."

I didn't know where I was, I didn't know what time it was, or even what day it was.

"Where am I?"

"A hospital in Newcastle."

"What? Why?"

"I don't want you to panic, I'll tell you later. I'm just glad you're awake."

"No, dad, tell me what happened. Please. I need to know. Where is Romeo?"

"He's outside in the waiting room- he'll come in a minute. I needed to speak to you alone."

"Ok, I'm sorry about everything dad. I shouldn't have ran off like that. It was stupid- and look how I ended up. You were right all along, I should have listened to you."

"No, I'm sorry. I should have never kicked you out. And I want to make it up to you, but I also need to protect you. So, you're going to have to come home- I can't have you being hurt again. We almost lost you."

What did he mean? Almost lost me? No one was telling me anything. I wanted people to be honest with me about what was going on.

"What do you mean?"

"I can't tell you now- we'll talk about it later."

"No, you have to tell me. I can't wait."

"Well- you had a bleed to the brain, something to do with impact."

"Impact of what? Is the baby ok?"

"I don't know how to say this…"

"Just tell me."

"They put you in emergency labour, to try and save the baby. The baby was born without complications and rushed into an incubator. But there is good news."

"Ok…"

"The baby was actually born at twenty-eight weeks and not at twenty-two weeks, like you thought.
But I'm sorry Nic, they don't know if she'll survive."

"She? It's a girl?"

"Yes."

It was bittersweet: I was over the moon that I was having a

girl, but she was born in such awful circumstances. This was all my fault- I had put this child through so much, and she hadn't even been born.

I was going to make sure she survived.

*

Romeo walked into the room, "Oh Nicola. Are you alright?"

"Hi Romeo. I'm fine. I can't really remember what happened though."

"I'm so, so sorry Nicola. This is all my fault. I promised to protect you and then this happened"

"It's not- you didn't know it would happen. It was bad timing- don't blame yourself."

"I do though- they may have never broken in if I had been there. I don't think it's safe for you to live here. I have made a massive mistake."

"What do you mean?" I glanced up at him- I was confused.

"I've put you in terrible danger. People will be after you because you're associated with me. They're trying to get to me."

"Who? What?"

"I can feel it, I don't know who, but the danger is not going to stop until they've got what they want.

You can't come back with me to Newcastle, Nicola. I'm so sorry, but it's not safe."

I was shocked at what I was hearing, but he was right. I needed to go- I can't raise my daughter in fear.

"I'm going to give you a bit of money so you'll be alright: a hundred thousand at least, but my accountant will sort it out."
"No Romeo, that's way too much. I could never take that from you."
"Please take it Nicola. I want you to be alright. Find a place to live somewhere else, somewhere away from all of this."
"Romeo, Thank you." I gave him a hug, and he left the room swiftly.

That was the last time I ever saw Romeo. A letter with a check came through my door a few weeks later.
And that was it.

23

The door creaked open. I shot up out of bed- it was the
nurse.

"You can go see her now."

"Oh my, I can't wait."

I followed the nurse towards a room, which had maybe a
dozen babies all lying in incubators. Immediately, my eyes
were drawn to one. I could tell it was mine because of all
the wires she was hooked up to, but she had the most
electric green eyes I had ever seen. She only had a small
strand of hair, but she was the most beautiful baby I'd ever
seen.

"This is your one." The nurse said to me, "Isn't she
gorgeous."

"Yes. She's perfect"

"Have you thought of any names?"

"I think I'm going to call her Valencia- it means warrior.
And she fought for her life, so I think it's fitting."

"I love that name!" The nurse replied. "Is there a father we
can call?"

"No, I'm going to raise this baby all on my own.
I don't need anyone's help."

THE END

Thank You

Thank you to everyone who bought and read this book, it means a lot. I knew this book had to be different to the first one, so I stripped it right back and changed the whole format. It's taken me a year to get here, but I'm so happy I can finally share this with you all.

I want to say thank you to my editor Ellie for making this all come to life.

Thank you to all my friends (especially Bonnie who let me base a whole character on her).

What Is To Come?

This definitely is not the end of Nicola's story; she will be back.

I think I'll do a sequel to this book next year, but I have other things I want to do before then, I definitely want to do another book before the end of this year. I'll try to do one with fewer dramas next time. (Not!)

Every time I try again to fake it

Know it gets a little harder

And harder to mean what I say

Lord, I know my heart, it just can't take it

And it beats a little harder

It gets harder to go my own way

Ain't nothing more to say

I know it's better if my heart breaks

Pixie Lott

Printed in Great Britain
by Amazon

38322934R00121